Death is the Pits

by

Suzanne Rossi

Death is the Pits

Cover Art by *Debbie Taylor*

The Wild Rose Press, Inc.
PO Box 708
Adams Basin, NY 14410-0708
Visit us at www.thewildrosepress.com

Publishing History
First Crimson Rose Edition, 2014
Print ISBN 978-1-61217-266-0
Digital ISBN 978-1-61217-267-7

Published in the United States of America

The pit relief glanced at his watch and scowled. I looked at my own. It read a three-oh-five. Greg was five minutes late. Very unusual. During the hubbub, I'd forgotten he'd been on break.

Another minute ticked by. The relief paced, his brows drawn together. Finally, Greg rushed in. His face was pale and his hands shaking.

"Sorry, I'm late, but the power outage caused a few accidents in the back. I was helping people."

The relief gave him the rundown on events and left.

"What happened backstage?" I asked.

He wiped his lips with a trembling hand. "What? Oh, backstage? A couple of staffers walked into doors and two people ran into each other with full trays of food, then slipped in the mess and fell. Time got away from me."

"Are you all right? You don't look so good."

He shot me an irritated glance. "I'm fine. It's been a long two days. I'm tired. Hope Graveyard gets here on time. Watch your games before Surveillance calls down with a problem. No need to spoil a clean night."

"Yeah, sure," I answered a bit put off by his brusque tone. I followed his orders anyway even though questions burned a hole in my tongue.

A few minutes later, a patron raced from the men's room near us and stopped at the entrance to Pit One, yelling, "Help! Help! He's dead!"

Praise for Suzanne Rossi

"I found *ALONG CAME QUINN* entertaining and a quick read. It's a fun road romance with a twist on the treasure that I think is different yet believable. And it just goes to show that sometimes you can't see what's right under your nose."

~ Dear Author

"I couldn't wait to turn each page to see what would happen next. Suzanne Rossi has definitely been added to my must-read list. The terrific twist on the run of the mill mob story makes *ALL IN THE FAMILY* a definite keeper."

~Theresa Joseph, The Romance Studio

"*A TANGLED WEB* has to be THE BEST romantic/suspenseful/mystery novel that I have read to date. The love scenes were perfectly timed with the plot, the suspense kept me turning the pages, and the mystery was superbly developed. Once I started reading it, I could not stop."

~Happily Ever After Reviews

"*NEARLY DEPARTED* is the BEST ghost story I have read in a long time. The wacky cast of characters is so colorful and fun that they bring the story to life."

~Night Owl Reviews

"I really got a good laugh out of *HEAR NO EVIL* and enjoyed the plot immensely which draws you in from the beginning... This author has done an incredible job penning this amazing tale."

~The Romance Studio

Dedication

I've heard it said that authors should write what they know, so in this case I took the advice. Several years ago, I was a dealer and then a floor supervisor for a casino in Northwest Mississippi.

The characters in this book are a mix of the many people I worked with there. A little bit of one, a smidgeon of another turned into Greg and Cassie. A huge part of me is in Dallas. I learned a lot from my real-life mentors who always lent a helping hand to a middle-aged woman who knew she was in over her head.

I want to especially thank fellow floor supervisors Carolyn Siegal and Zee Bower along with pit manager Jerry Bower for all their support. Without them I'd never have lasted as long as I did at the job. You guys were, and still are, the best!

Chapter One

Calling shift manager Tina Rosetti a bitch was a gross understatement. She had the reputation of patting a dealer, a floor supervisor, and even a pit manager on the back one minute, and writing him or her up the next, often with a royal ass-chewing. It was my bad luck to have just been the recipient of the latter. A twenty-dollar overpayment by one of the dealers in my section had added to my collection of pink slips.

Pit manager, Greg Holland, looked at me with raised eyebrows when I re-entered Pit Two of the Casablanca Casino in Terence, Mississippi. I stomped past him and approached dealer Cliff Edwards, the object of my still smarting rear end. He dealt at a snail's pace to a full table on a three-dollar game.

"Go see Tina on your next break," I said in his ear.

He shot me a glance. "Why? Did I do something wrong?"

Did Cliff the Klutz ever do anything right? "How many pink slips do you have over the past few months for overpayments?"

"Uh, three."

"Well, you're about to get number four, which means you'll have three days to call your own starting tomorrow."

"I'm getting suspended?"

"What do you think?"

I turned and left him, heading back to the pit stand.

"Change a hundred," one of the dealers called out.

I glanced over at table fifteen. At least Ellen knew how to count out a hundred bucks worth of checks.

"Change it."

"You look like you're ready to hurt somebody," Greg said. "What happened?"

Greg Holland was an all-around nice guy and my former lover. We'd met at a party a little over three years ago. I was a dealer at the Casablanca and he was a pit manager at the Lucky Deal. The attraction—at least on my part—was instantaneous. Our affair was all fire and I fell hard for the guy. My imagination soared to the future, something I rarely let happen. Past busted relationships had left me gun shy, and swing shift hours didn't allow much in the line of socialization. Until Greg, that is.

We sizzled for three months until one night when he dropped a bomb on me. We'd just finished making love. He got up and dressed while I lazed in the bed, satiated with the afterglow of great sex. Then he'd told me it was over—no real explanation, just that we were through. Emotional pain had slashed my chest. I wanted to cry, scream and beg him to reconsider, but a crumb of self-respect forced me to lift my chin and pretend to accept his decision. I worked hard to keep the tears at bay.

I'd gone home and cried for two days. My life had been shattered, but try as I might, I couldn't hate Greg. For the next few weeks I went to work, did my job, and managed to come to grips that I'd most likely never see or hear from him again. By the end of three months, I'd begun to heal.

Then one night, I walked into Pit Two and there he was standing at the pit podium. My breath had caught somewhere in my throat threatening to choke me. He looked up and smiled. I knew instantly I'd only been fooling myself into believing it was over.

Greg was fun to be around, friendly, and kept things on a professional basis, although the past couple of months I'd begun to wonder. Little glances, the occasional touch, and the ability to always be near me during breaks, told me that maybe he was changing his mind.

Worked for me. As I said, I'd never completely gotten over him.

"Dallas! Yoohoo! Anybody home? I asked you a question."

Greg's voice brought me out of my memories and back to the business at hand.

I tossed the folded pink paper onto the pit podium. "Give you one guess."

"Shit, Dallas, what did you do now?"

"Old Cliff changed a hundred a little while ago and gave out a hundred and twenty. When's he going to learn that changing a hundred is four stacks of *five* nickel checks, not six? I was replacing the cards on table sixteen and okayed it. My fault. I should have checked closer knowing he can't count worth a damn. How the hell does he stayed employed?"

"Who the hell changes a hundred on a three-dollar table?"

"Someone who realizes the mistake and leaves after playing one hand."

"What did Tina have to say?"

I shrugged. "The usual—I'm incompetent,

unobservant, and only have my job because management wanted another female floor supervisor. She also said if I wanted to keep the job, to toe the line, and cut down on break room rhetoric and criticism of the casino."

Greg snorted. "She should talk. The only reason she's shift manager is because her last name ends in a vowel and it's rumored her husband's uncle has Mafia ties in Atlantic City. And the real reason you got written up was because of the criticism."

"Change five hundred!"

Not my table, thank God. The floor supervisor called out the okay to change five, while Greg eyeballed the transaction making sure the dealer handed out the correct amount and denomination of checks in exchange for the cash, and then turned back to me. "Better go keep an eye on your tables. It's Saturday night."

Yeah, Saturday night, one of the busiest of the week. Suckers beat the doors down in a misguided effort to increase their recently cashed paychecks. To them it was easier than winning the lottery. Casino workers referred to this as the Redneck Retirement Plan. Swing shift had barely begun. So far, this Saturday night sucked.

I was in charge of five tables—a roulette game, and four featuring blackjack. Other than Cliff, the rest of my dealers knew how to pull cards and spin a wheel. I had developed the ability to watch the cash flow and the cards with reasonable enough accuracy, while thinking of other subjects at the same time—like Greg.

Much as I hated to admit it, Tina was right about one thing. I wasn't the best floor supervisor to come down the pike. This lower rung management position wasn't as satisfying as I'd expected. I'd go back to dealing in a heartbeat, but couldn't afford the pay cut. Funny how easy it is to accept the increase and how hard it is to adjust to the opposite. I didn't have the experience a supervisory position required, but here in Terence, few people did. Most were a step or two above their competence levels, including the casino manager, Howard Spivey.

To the best of anyone's knowledge, he'd never been a floor supervisor or a pit manager, although he did know how to play craps and blackjack. I wasn't even sure he knew how to deal. We took bets back in the break room on who he'd blackmailed into giving him the position. Obviously, the Mississippi Gaming Commission didn't give a shit.

By the time my break rolled around, the crowd had increased. Most of my tables were full. Thankfully, I had no big spenders in my section. With the exception of the three-dollar table and roulette, the rest were all nickels, casino slang for a five-dollar minimum bet.

My relief, Rudy Gantry, signed in and I escaped to the break room. I snagged a soda along with a candy bar from the vending machines, and grabbed a chair at one of the tables where I could forget about my shortcomings and daydream about Greg.

In spite of our break up, daydreaming about him had become an almost full time occupation lately. Those mind trips had kept the hope alive that someday we might get back together, although if I was honest with myself, hope was about all I had. And those little fantasies weren't chaste. I remembered the reality all too vividly. Sometimes I found it hard to look him in the eye in the break room or the pit. But what was really strange was that sometimes he'd look at me like he *knew*! Silly, of course, but disconcerting nonetheless.

"Hear you bought pink again, Daniels," one of the box men in the craps pit said with a smirk bringing me out of fantasyland.

I pushed Greg to the back of my mind. "Yeah, two more and I can finally paper that bathroom." I opened the soda and drank, enjoying the laughter my comment evoked.

"A write-up should not be trivialized or a source of amusement."

"Cram it up your ass, Ralph," one of the craps dealers said.

I sniggered. Ralph Klinger was known as Ralph the Rat. A floor supervisor, usually in the craps pit, he had a superior, sanctimonious attitude. His baby face didn't go with the tall frame, which was already running to fat. Not a good image for someone in his early thirties. I'd recently read where Mississippi was ranked number one in the country for obesity. At least, it was number one in something. I shook my head and turned my thoughts back to Ralph. The little weasel was also a snitch. He eavesdropped on every conversation he could, and then tattled to management with any negative remarks.

Ralph glared at the offending dealer and left the room walking upright as though he had a broomstick up his ass.

"Guess you'll be visiting Tina's office, too," I said, unwrapping the candy bar and taking a huge bite.

"Like I give a shit. An engineering firm in Memphis called this afternoon. I got the job I interviewed for last week. This dump is history."

A pang of envy swept over me. Lucky bastard. He had a real job. He'd get to spend weekends and holidays with his family, not sweating over a dice table crowded with twenty gamblers all in various stages of inebriation.

And don't forget sleep. He'll actually enjoy a decent sleep pattern.

The rest of the world revolves around nine-to-five, but casinos operate twenty-four-seven. I hated going to bed at five in the morning, and then pretending two in the afternoon was a normal time to wake up. I won't even get into how the hours screwed up my internal clock on my days off.

One of the blackjack dealers wandered over and pulled out a chair. Her name was Doris and not only could she count accurately, but she dealt cards with blazing speed. I loved flooring her because she rarely made a mistake, and if she did, owned up to it immediately. In other words, I trusted her and didn't have to keep my eyes peeled to catch errors like I did with Cliff. Made my job a hell of a lot easier.

"Hey, Doris, what's happening? Where they got you tonight?" I asked.

"Pit One on a nickel table."

"A nickel game? You? What a stupid waste of talent."

Only Tina the Warrior Princess would put a cracking good dealer like Doris on a nickel table when the twenty-five dollar game was packed. She shuffled that shoe every five to six minutes. The more hands dealt; the more money the casino made. Even I knew that.

"Tell me," she said with an earnest expression. "Is

there a full moon tonight?"

"I don't know. Why?"

"I've got every nutcase and weirdo in the tri-state area on my table. One idiot insisted on hitting a seventeen, and then got pissed when he busted. Another spilled his beer all over the shoe, and we had to switch out cards after only three hands. And then there's the moron who splits tens, and calls it bad luck when I pull a seven to a fourteen. Oh, and I also have some coked-out babe trolling for off-table action."

"I attracted serial killers and ax murderers when I dealt. Guess my luck passed on to you."

"Them I can deal with," she said with a glance at her watch. "Damn, where does twenty minutes go?" She rose. "See you later."

I still had time left on my break and was in no hurry to return to the pit. In the five years I'd worked at the Casablanca, I'd watched it go from a promising career to wondering how to get out of the business and still make the same amount of money. So far, I hadn't found the solution.

I crammed the last of the candy bar into my mouth and washed it down with the soda. It would tide me over until my next break an hour and a half from now.

Out of the corner of my eye, I saw Ralph the Rat casually lounging against the wall in the smoking room, no doubt eavesdropping on the unsuspecting smokers huddled around the table a few feet away. He waved his hand to send the spiraling cigarette smoke away from his face.

Come on, Ralph, is lung cancer from second-hand smoke really worth that brief moment of praise from Tina?

The sad part was Ralph didn't have to suck up to advance his career. He was a damned good dealer. He knew all the games, which meant he could either deal or supervise in all pits. A shift manager's dream come true. So, why spy on his co-workers?

Before I could formulate an answer, Cliff walked up clutching a pink slip with a puzzled expression on his face.

"Going home, Cliff?" I tried to keep the eagerness from my voice.

"No, not yet." He handed me the slip. "Does this make any sense to you?"

Jay Colter, a boxman from the craps pit paused behind me and read over my shoulder.

"What the hell is a working suspension?" he asked.

"I have no idea." I looked up at my dealer. "Did Tina give any explanation?"

Cliff scratched his head. "Sort of. She said the suspension would go into my record, but I'd continue to work."

"You're either suspended or you're not," the boxman replied. "I've never heard of this."

I handed the paper back. "Sounds to me like another scam by management to screw us over. You know, a black mark in the record book, but still making you work. Are you getting paid?"

"I guess," Cliff replied with a shrug.

"Be just like the cheap bastards to let you keep tokes, but screw you out of salary because technically, you're on suspension. Come on, Dallas, time to go to work," Jay said.

Back in the pit, I signed on my games, and then glanced at Greg when he sidled up next me. His close presence made concentrating on my job harder. I took a deep breath to settle my nerves.

"Everything all right?" he asked.

"Uh, yeah, fine."

He smiled a slow smile and lowered his left eyelid in a half-wink.

Oh crap! He knows!

I shifted my gaze to one of the BJ tables and rubbed the back of my neck.

"Neck hurt? Turn around."

I turned and he gently massaged my neck. My heart rate accelerated, my breath clogged my throat, and my knees went weak. I prayed I wouldn't collapse onto the pit floor. Was this a subtle overture to renewing our relationship? I had no clue and didn't know what to think.

Nora Nelson, the pit relief, waddled in. She eyed us but said nothing. Greg ceased his actions and stepped back. I hurried toward the roulette game. I didn't need to hear Nora's caustic comments.

Seven-and-a-half-months pregnant, she looked enormous and was hormonal as hell. Normal Nora was a bitch, but Knocked-Up Nora sent even the most hardened casino employee running for cover. Statuesque, her long dark hair and slightly slanted dark eyes—suggesting Asian ancestry at some point in time—gave her an exotic appearance.

She'd been flooring the Caribbean Stud tables a couple of weeks ago when the hapless pit manager accidentally gave her the wrong colored cards to change out. The next thing he knew, the boxes had flown back through the air with Nora screaming, "I said purple, goddammit!" Fortunately, her aim sucked.

Nora was one of those people who feared nothing and no one. Cutting her career teeth in Vegas, she'd seen it all and done most of it herself. With the tongue of an adder, she didn't care who she sliced and diced, and didn't suffer fools gladly, which meant she hated Tina, Howard—neither of whom had the guts to reprimand her for anything—and damn near everybody else in the joint. For some reason, she liked me, Greg, and Cassie Severin. What the hell she was doing in Terence was anybody's guess, and no one dared ask.

As Greg left on his break, she turned to me. "Heard that asshole Tina wrote you up again," she said, not bothering to lower her voice.

"Yeah, me and Cliff."

"Cliff I can see. He's the dumbest excuse for a dealer I've ever seen. Must be somebody's relative."

We only stood a few feet away from Cliff's table. He heard and shot a hurt glance over his shoulder toward Nora. Swell, now I'd have to deal with the aftermath of her remark.

"You ever heard of a working suspension?"

"A working what?" I told her. She shook her head and sneered. "Those stinking bastards will do anything to save a buck and their sorry asses. I'll tell you what happened. Tina probably approved the early out list before she saw the tape of Cliff screwing up and hasn't got anyone to replace him, so she and that horse's ass Spivey made up a working suspension as some kind of new money-making scheme to present to headquarters. What do you want?" she snapped at a floor from the Stud section.

"Uh, we have a flush on table two."

"Ah, shit! Couldn't the son of a bitch have waited

until I was out of the pit?"

Nora stalked off behind the floor, and I returned to watching my tables. A flush was a good thing for a player, but the Casablanca was paranoid over losing money. As a result anything over three-of-a-kind needed a pit manager's supervision. It was a pain in the ass since flushes and straights weren't uncommon. No one liked flooring those carnival games.

It was a busy Saturday, and for the next ninety minutes I stayed occupied with my games, but was glad when Rudy walked into the pit.

The first person I saw in the break room was Cassie Severin, my mentor and friend. No one knew Cassie's real age—she kept that to herself. However, one night she slipped and made a comment about looking forward to retirement. Eventually, I learned she'd started as a dealer in Reno thirty-five years ago. I did the math and came up with a ballpark figure of between fifty-five and sixty.

She didn't look it. Her dark hair showed no gray and her skin remained miraculously unwrinkled. To the best of my knowledge, she didn't use hair color or Botox. On the tall side, she boasted a remarkable figure. Cassie swore everything was natural.

I hit the vending machines again, and then carted my candy and soda over to her table.

"Hey, girl, where have you been? Haven't seen you all night," I commented, popping the top on the can and unwrapping another chocolate fix.

To my surprise, she scowled and blurted, "That fucking bitch. I swear I'll kill her."

Chapter Two

I stopped with the candy bar halfway to my mouth and stared in surprise. Cassie usually dealt with anger and frustration by engaging in biting, humor-laced sarcasm. It had gotten her into trouble on more than one occasion. Her pink slip count rivaled mine. Greg Holland placed a close third.

"Which bitch?" Given the hierarchy of the Casablanca management, her reference could be to one of several.

"That back-stabbing troll! I swear if she had balls, I'd string her up by them." Cassie yanked a napkin from the holder on the table and proceeded to rip it into shreds.

"I take it you're talking about our esteemed shift manager, Tina." I chomped into my Mars bar.

"Who the hell else?"

"What did she do to you this time? She write you up again, too?"

"Two months ago, I put in for next weekend off. My granddaughter is graduating from Cal Tech—Cal Tech, for God's sake. My request was approved. I've got the plane tickets, and am halfway packed. So, what do I see when I come in tonight? My name on next week's schedule. I go back before shift and tell her she's goofed. Know what she says?"

I swigged soda. "You can't have the time off?"

She shoved the pile of scraps to the side and grabbed another napkin. "Said she had no record of my request and she's short floors."

"Why is she short floors?"

"Because Charlie-The-Ass-Kisser wants that weekend off, too."

Cassie referred to Charlene Bates. A Terence native, she had worked at the first casino opened down here, and with her long blonde hair, big blue eyes, and forty-inch chest had been hired as a floor supervisor by Spivey. Speculation ran rife on how she actually got the job. Most of us figured she killed time staring at the ceiling. Charlene wasn't quite the rat Ralph was, but she sucked up to anyone who could give her power. Rumor had it she was next in line for a dual-rate pit manager position. I swore if she got it, I was out of here.

"Let me guess, she made this request just recently?"

"Two days ago from what I hear."

"Knowing Tina, she forgot she'd okayed yours and agreed to give Charlie the time off, too. If Tina rescinds Charlie's okay, the little worm will go crying to Spivey, who will insist on the time off being re-instated. In other words, he screws you."

Cassie snorted. "No, he screws Charlene; he just fucks me over."

I took another bite of candy and noticed Ralph Klinger seated at the table next to us. I was sure he had his ears fine tuned to the conversation, especially since Cassie didn't bother to lower her voice.

"Tina the Warrior Princess has no business being a shift manager. She doesn't know what she's doing and has no people skills whatsoever. I heard she never floored or pitted in Atlantic City, but moved directly to this position because of family ties—and I do mean *family*. Shit, the stupid cow doesn't have a working knowledge of craps either."

Ralph rose and left the room.

"Cassie, you may want to tone it down. Ralph the Rat overheard you and just took off, no doubt to Tina's office."

"Who gives a shit? I've had it with this place. Do you know where I am tonight? I'm on a stinking two-hour rotation in Pit One. How many times have I asked not to be placed on a two hour? My knees won't take it."

No one liked flooring in Pit One. Pits Two and Four had twelve to fifteen tables each. Pit Three contained six craps tables. All ran parallel to each other. But for some reason, Pit One was perpendicular to the rest and boasted four roulette games. The others were all blackjack for a total of twenty-one. No way could three floors handle the setup, even at this place, so on the weekends when all the games were open, a fourth floor supervisor was added. This pushed the breaks back to once every two hours as opposed to the usual ninety minute intervals.

To people outside the business, getting a half hour break every two hours sounds like heaven, but take my word, it's not. The job demands concentration, and the longer a floor is in the pit, the less concentration. Mistakes are made. Mistakes cost the casino money and buy the floor supervisor a write-up. I should know.

"So what are you going to do?"

Cassie raised her head and sneered. "I'm going on

my fucking vacation. And while I'm in Pasadena, I plan on taking a side trip to Laughlin or maybe even Las Vegas. I'll apply at every casino in Nevada if I have to. I can still deal."

"Go bitch to human resources. They'll intervene. You'll be released from floor duties, and get to see your granddaughter graduate. Not even Tina or Howard can override an HR decision. Take it easy. Don't pop a blood vessel. We all know Tina's a moron. Eventually, not even her connections will keep her employed. The mob's not fond of morons who lose money."

"Maybe." She stopped shredding napkins and gazed at me for the first time. "I'm sorry, I haven't even asked how you're doing. Where are you tonight?"

"Cheapskate end of Pit Two—a three-dollar table, three nickels, and roulette. Could be worse."

"Yeah, you could be in Pit One and on two-hour rotations."

At least she said it with a smile. I finished my candy and slurped the last of my soda. I was still hungry, but would eat real food from the employees' cafeteria during my next break.

"So, wanna go to the Southern Belle after shift?" I asked. "I got lucky a couple of weeks ago. Won a hundred bucks."

"I don't know. It depends on how pissed I still am. Never gamble when you're drinking or pissed."

"If that's the case, I wonder why any of us hit the tables."

My friend rose. "You're right. I've still got time left on my break. I think I'll head upstairs and talk to HR. See you later."

"Ask for Jennifer Hayden. She's not real fond of

Tina from what I hear."

Cassie nodded and left. I was relieved she'd calmed down. I'd seen her formidable temper, usually held in check, unleashed a couple of times—once when she'd called Cliff a stupid asshole while he was still on the table, and once in the break room. She and Charlene had gone at it. I'm not sure how the argument started, but I do know Cassie questioned Charlene's morals, although I always considered the phrase "fucking whore" to be redundant. My friend had gathered a pink slip on each occasion.

Nora was in the pit when I signed back onto my games.

"Am I late?" I asked.

"Naw, they pulled me out of the craps pit to cover here for a few minutes."

"Why? Where's Greg?"

"In with the warrior and the snake." She used her own terminology for Tina and Spivey.

"Oh, shit, what's he done now?"

Greg's idea of fun was to make outrageous comments with a straight face, so the recipient couldn't decide if he'd just been insulted or complimented. His use of sarcasm rivaled Cassie's. I envied them both the ability. I'm afraid I just call a spade a spade with little or no subtlety. Diplomacy was not my strong suit.

Nora shrugged. "I have no idea, but the call came a few minutes ago. Karl Hamilton's watching over pits three and four. Whatever it is, it must be a pisser. They didn't even wait to fuck me out of my break time."

The few minutes stretched into twenty. Nora spent most of that time glancing at her watch and scowling. Her break time neared. I minded my own business and kept an eagle eye on BJ 21. A drunk with more money than ability had hit a losing streak. I expected an eruption any moment. Drunks and assholes did that— lost, and then yelled at the dealer like it was their fault.

I also monitored the roulette game closely. Two regulars I'd nicknamed Goofy and Daffy had wandered up. A few weeks ago, they insisted they lost because the surveillance camera was really a laser, and then accused the dealer of pressing a hidden button to activate it, thus making the ball jump from one number to another.

Maybe Doris is right. There has to be a full moon.

Mark Davis, the craps pit manager, walked past returning from his break with raised eyebrows when he saw Nora in Pit Two. She shook her head and frowned deeper. He moved on.

"All right, now the bastards are on my time. What the hell kind of a reaming can take this long?"

Five minutes later, Greg returned. I wanted to ask what had gone down, but one look at his face and the question died on my lips. He looked ready to kill.

"It's about time," Nora snapped. "This is cutting into my break."

"So, quit whining and take your goddamned break."

She gaped at him, whirled on her heel, and then left. I'd never seen Nora speechless or Greg so furious. His pale face and red cheeks told me something major had gone down. He busied himself at the pit stand for a couple of minutes, and then strode over to me.

"Anything I should know about in your section?" His tone was ice cold and the words clipped.

I'd never heard *him* like this before. For once, no hot fantasy crowded my mind.

"Just a drunk on table twenty-one and the camera-is-really-a-laser couple on roulette. I can handle it."

"Good." He turned and approached floor supervisor Mary Winslow's section.

Whatever had happened, Greg didn't intend sharing. I glanced at my watch—another hour until my break. I sighed. No doubt about it, this was going to be a long night.

A new customer sat down at one of the blackjack tables. I took his player's card and checked him in at the pit stand. Mary sidled over while Greg dealt with a payout on Caribbean Stud.

"Whew! I've never seen Greg so pissed. Wonder what happened. He say anything to you?"

"Not a word and I'm not asking. He'll tell us sooner or later." I clocked my player in and wished him good luck.

"Floor!"

I closed my eyes. It was Michelle, my roulette dealer. I heaved a breath and walked over.

"Yes, Michelle?" She didn't speak, but pointed to Goofy—or maybe it was Daffy. The names were interchangeable. Of medium height and skinny, tonight he wore what I'd come to call his casino clothes—a pair of blue, red, and yellow paisley-print slacks and a Kelly green T-shirt. His wife's mousey brown hairstyle reminded me of Moe Howard of the Three Stooges fame. Built like a fireplug, this evening she dressed in a pair of short-shorts and a tank top—both several sizes too small. She looked like a discount store moment ready to hit the internet.

"Yes, sir, is there a problem?"

"Turn off the laser or I'll sue," he demanded.

"Sir, we've been through this before. There is no laser." I tried to sound polite, but the absurdness of it all made me want to laugh, and when I want to laugh, it's hard to suppress the urge.

"I have a system. I play the same twenty-eight numbers on every spin. It can't fail. So far I've played ten spins and haven't won a dime. This game is rigged."

That was a system? The laughter moved from my chest to my throat. I swallowed in the hope it would disappear before it burst from my mouth.

"Sir, I'd like to point out that there are *thirty*-eight numbers on the board, which means ten are uncovered." I felt my lips twitch. I was losing it. Like I said—no subtlety or diplomacy in my blood.

"You find this funny? I want your supervisor. Now!"

I had no choice. I motioned Greg over. He didn't need an explanation. He knew—just like he seemed to know a lot of things.

"Back to the laser business again?"

"Uh-huh."

"Change two hundred!" I moved away to okay the transaction, and then hurried back. No way did I want to miss anything.

"I don't know why I come in here!" Goofy/Daffy shouted.

Yeah, I couldn't figure that one out either. What kind of an idiot bets at a place he thinks is cheating him?

"Sir, there are ten casinos in Terence," Greg replied, his tone not friendly.

"And I'm going to one of them now—after I lodge a formal complaint with your casino manager." He and his wife walked away.

"Did you take their money?" I asked Michelle.

"Every last dollar."

"Maybe now you can turn off the laser," a customer from the far end of the table said with a grin.

All of us, except Greg, laughed.

"Change a hundred," Cliff called. I hurried over to make sure that's what he handed out.

The night wore on. I ate dinner on my next break, and later spied Cassie heading for the office. I supposed her tirade had been reported.

Or maybe the trip to HR worked and she's being granted her request after all.

By two o'clock the warbling notes of the slots being played along with the clang of coins hitting the trays, and cheers from the craps pit blotted out all other sounds. Greg was still uncommunicative, and I didn't have time to ask questions.

Nora waddled in to relieve Greg, a sour look on her face. I avoided her. Luckily she spent the first few minutes in the Stud area, also known as the P. T. Barnum Memorial Section of Pit Two. Eventually, she wandered down my way. A look of pain had replaced the sour one.

"Are you all right?" I asked.

"No," she snapped back. "My feet hurt, my back hurts, my ankles look like cantaloupes, and that bitch called me on the carpet for a discussion."

"A discussion? You mean she wrote you up?"

"Get real. She wouldn't dare. I'd take her pen and jam it up her ass. No, she called it a little chat about being polite to fellow workers."

"Tonight must be the night for it. What did you

do?"

"Told Charlene to quit acting like a hooker flirting with the customers and watch her games. She complained to Tina I was abusive. If she wants abusive, I'll give her abusive. She ain't *begun* to see abusive yet. Bitches, both of them."

Tina walk passed Pit Two on her way to Pit Three, the usual large travel mug of coffee in her hand. Her dark, blunt cut, shoulder length hair swung against her face with each step. The style reminded me of an ancient Egyptian princess. At six feet, two inches, she exuded quite an impressive presence, hence the backroom nickname of Warrior Princess.

"There she goes on her nightly appearance in the craps pit to pretend she knows what she's doing," Nora said with a sneer.

"Probably learning the game." Actually, that wasn't far from the case.

Tina gulped a huge amount of coffee and set the mug on the pit stand, and then paraded up and down, glancing over the boxmen's shoulders at the action. I gazed at the show with contempt.

"Change hundred!"

I okayed the transaction and spent the next ten or fifteen minutes doing my job before once again casting my eyes toward the craps pit and the incompetent Tina.

Suddenly, she placed a hand to her chest, or maybe it was her throat—I couldn't see all that well, and staggered toward the pit clerk's chair. Before anybody could do much of anything, she collapsed onto the floor.

Chapter Three

"Holy shit!" I cried at the same instant the pit clerk screamed.

The noise level lowered for a second, and then patrons fled nearby tables and slot machines to see what the commotion was all about. Nora stared, but said nothing. I think she was too stunned. Security raced into Pit Three. Surveillance must have called them.

"Color coming in," one of my dealers called out, bringing me back to my job. Nothing save fire or tornados stops the action, and sometimes not even that. I had firsthand knowledge of this. One night the fire alarms went off. Whoop, whoop, whoop complete with flashing lights. Not a single player moved. The only way they'd leave was if flames were licking their asses on the seats.

"Bring it in," I called.

The dealer cut out three hundred dollars' worth of checks. I okayed it, and she pushed it toward the customer.

"What's going on over there?" she asked beginning her deal again.

"Looks like Tina tripped and fell."

"Probably over her own stupidity."

Greg returned and gazed over at the craps pit, too. "What's that all about?"

"I have no idea. All I know is I'm on break.

Nothing's going on," Nora reported and left.

The crowd around Pit Three was ten deep with people jumping up and down to get a better look. Spivey, his spare tire jiggling, trotted past Pit Two with a worried look.

"Change twenty."

"Cliff, you don't have to ask permission to change twenty bucks," I reminded him.

"Dallas, Mary, Rich, watch your tables," Greg ordered. He paced up and down the pit tossing an occasional glance in the direction of Pit Three.

I sneaked a quick peek at him. His face remained pale and his hands shook slightly. Whatever had gone down earlier still had him upset and furious.

The crowd around the craps pit thinned and players returned to other activities, the lure of easy money more attractive than someone laid out on the pit floor. Every few seconds, I shot a look across the aisle to watch the progress. So far, Tina was still down. The paramedics burst through the front doors and ran toward her.

"This must be damned serious if they've called an ambulance," I commented.

"Who cares? As long as she's off my back," Greg snapped. "Keep an eye on BJ nineteen. Centerfield looks familiar. I think he was in here capping bets last week."

A cheer rose from one of the craps tables and I heard the stick man make his call. "Seven, winner seven. Take the don'ts and pay the line."

As I said, nothing interrupted a hot game. With Greg still not ready to share information about his trip to the woodshed, I did as he asked and kept my eye on the man sitting in the center spot on table nineteen. He looked up and smiled knowing I watched his actions. I moved on. Sooner or later he'd try to add more checks to the stack after the cards had been dealt.

I proceeded to watch my games, glancing over to Pit Three every once in a while where the paramedics still worked on Tina. They spent close to half an hour doing whatever it is they do before standing. A gurney was wheeled into the pit.

"Change two hundred."

I turned my gaze to BJ seventeen. "Change it."

The dealer waved a player's card in the air and I checked the woman in at the pit stand. Greg was in the Stud section with a payoff.

"What's going on over there?" she asked as I returned the card.

"I think someone fainted. Here's your card. Good luck."

When I looked over to the craps pit again, the gurney was leaving and the body on it was draped from head to toe in a red blanket.

"Son of a bitch! She's dead?" I said with a gasp.

Greg rejoined me at the pit stand and stared with a blank expression. Then, he smiled.

"Couldn't happen to a more deserving person," he said.

"Greg, you can't mean that," Anne Sherman, our pit clerk said, a nice lady who tended to see the best in people. She must have had to dig hard for that ability working in the Casablanca.

"I can and I do. Why defend her? She wrote you up yesterday."

"You got written up?" I asked in disbelief. Anne was the most conscientious pit clerk I'd ever met.

"What for?"

"I made a mistake with a fill and ordered three thousand in green instead of two. It had to go back and the game stopped because the dealer ran out of green checks."

"Ouch. Who was the pit manager?"

"Nancy Johnson. I felt awful. I'd never been written up before." Anne shook her head and her gaze followed Tina's body cart to the front doors.

I did the same. Few in the casino didn't watch. The pit phone rang and Greg answered. My head snapped around as he hung up swearing.

"Dammit, Dallas. I thought I told you to keep an eye on nineteen. Surveillance just called. Centerfield capped. Who's the dealer?"

Shit. I'd forgotten about him. "Ron Black."

"Go watch the game, and tell Ron to keep his eyes open. Don't let it happen again."

I hustled my ass back to nineteen and whispered the information into the dealer's ear. He nodded. Centerfield had taken advantage of the distraction of Tina's death roll toward the front doors to increase his winnings. Not stupid, the man had headed for the cashier as soon as the payoff hit the table. He was nowhere in sight.

I guess a body being wheeled out of the casino was the catalyst for calling it a night. Gamblers, a superstitious bunch, must have considered Tina's death bad karma. Two of my BJ tables had gone dead and only a smattering of players remained on the other two. Roulette had one player.

Greg wandered down my way. "Whew! What a night."

"You can say that again. I've never seen anyone die in a casino before."

"Used to happen all the time in Atlantic City. Those old geezers hoping to supplement their social security would win a couple of hundred, and about once a month one of them would keel over from excitement." He shook his head. "I remember one fat guy who dropped dead and fell over the velvet rope separating the pit from the casino floor. Landed on top of a floor supervisor. Pinned her right to the carpet. She thrashed and screamed for someone to get him off her. Looked like two wrestlers in the ring."

"What do you think happened to Tina?"

He shrugged. "Who knows? I'd say she had a heart attack, but that's not likely. She doesn't have a heart."

I sensed Greg might be ready to talk. "We all know that. No heart and no brain. Makes me feel like I walked into a surreal *Wizard of Oz*. You obviously got chewed out tonight, too. Wanna talk about it?"

"Not really, but let's just say that it was bad. I lost my temper with Tina and Howard. Told them what I thought of them, their competence levels, and this casino in general."

"Holy cow. What'd they do?"

"Don't know yet. I was supposed to meet with them after shift. I may have bought a permanent pink slip," he confessed.

"Good God Almighty! What did you say to them and why were you in there in the first place?"

"I'll tell you later. Think I'll go lose a little money at the Golden Hoard later. Want to come?"

I didn't really. I was tired and wanted to go to bed, but my curiosity overrode sleep.

"Sure. Cassie may come, too, if she's over her mad."

"Cassie's pissed? Swell, let's all meet and verbally trash this dump."

The night wound down. Another hour before Swing ended and Graveyard took over. I faced my playing tables, so Surveillance would think I was attentive.

Spivey still hovered in Pit Three having a heated discussion with the head of security, Dave Billings. The last of the paramedics packed up their gear. The pit phone rang and the pit manager answered, listened, hung up, said something to Spivey and the remaining EMTs. Our commanding general then raced from the pit with Billings and the paramedics on his heels. They made a beeline for the offices.

"Now what?" I asked Greg.

"I have no clue." He checked his watch. "All I know is my relief is due in less than twenty minutes."

Four of my five games had idle dealers who checked their watches and yawned awaiting the end of another night's work. Only Cliff's three-dollar table had players.

"Should we close any games?" I asked.

"Hell, no. Why create work for ourselves? Let Graveyard do it."

I spent the next ten minutes wandering around my section, chatting with the dealers and making sure Cliff didn't do something stupid to get me into hot water again with only a few minutes left on the evening.

I glanced back at the pit podium. Greg was on the phone, his eyebrows drawn together in a frown. He hung up and headed in my direction.

"You're not going to believe this. I just got a call from Spivey. All swing shift pit personnel are ordered to gather in the big meeting room on the second floor after shift. No exceptions."

"You gotta be kidding. What for?" Eight hours in this little slice of not quite heaven was long enough.

"It seems Spivey's secretary just dropped dead."

My jaw sagged. "You're kidding! What's going on? First Tina and now what's-her-name, Janet?"

"I have no idea, but Spivey is pulling tape on who came and went in the offices tonight, and has already called the cops."

"The cops?" I said with a gasp. "You mean someone thinks this is…" I couldn't say the word.

"Murder? I don't know, but it sure is suspicious."

Greg left to inform the other floor supervisors, while I told my dealers the orders, but not the reason. None were happy.

"My feet are killing me," Ellen Haskell complained. "If they want to talk to us about something, do it tomorrow before shift. What's going on?"

I shrugged. "We've been told to clock out and go upstairs. No exceptions. That's all I can tell you."

Greg's Graveyard relief, Don Hutchins, walked in and spoke with Greg for a few minutes. On his way out of the pit Greg stopped and murmured in my ear.

"Don told me cops are all over the employee parking lot and in the back area hallways. This is going to be interesting. I'll save you a seat."

He left, and I waited impatiently for my relief to show up. Finally, Betty Grayson sauntered in, signed onto my games, and then asked, "Anything I need to know?"

"Nope. All's quiet. I hear there's commotion in the back."

She rolled her eyes. "If cops are involved, you guys might not get out of here until noon."

On that cheerful note, I fled the responsibilities of Pit Two and clocked out. Cassie met me at the foot of the stairwell. We mounted the steps together.

"Is it true? Tina the Warrior Princess is dead?" she asked in a low voice.

"Either that or she's getting a body wrap courtesy of the Terence County Fire Rescue Squad. Apparently, Spivey's secretary bought the big one, too."

Cassie stopped climbing and stared with a shocked gaze. "Janet? Who'd want to hurt her? She's a nice lady even though she does work for an asshole."

I shook my head. I had a feeling Betty was right. Some of us wouldn't get out of here until well after sun-up.

The meeting room was a large area often used for dining when a convention or private party was booked into the casino hotel. Pit personnel for swing shift numbered over one hundred people. Not all of them would find seats at the dozen or so tables haphazardly set up. A group had used the room earlier in the evening. The buffet tables toward the rear of the room still bore several stacks of unused plates and bins of silverware.

Already pit managers, floor supervisors, and others who'd caught the early out had staked a claim on the available seating. Greg waved from across the room. Cassie and I hurried to join him.

"Any news?" I asked, plopping into a chair and

kicking my shoes off. I dug my toes into the carpeting.

"Not yet. When Spivey gets done with viewing the tapes, we'll know more. Hi, Cassie."

"Hi. What do you mean by viewing the tapes?"

"I guess they want to see who came and went in the office area tonight," he replied. "Maybe someone with a grudge decided to take it to another level."

"Someone with a grudge? That could refer to the whole fucking casino." Cassie yawned and put a hand to her throat. "I hope this doesn't take long. I'm tired and don't feel so hot. Those damned two-hour rotations make me physically sick."

"Well, if they're talking to anyone who entered the office tonight, the three of us will be here forever." I turned to Cassie. "Did you get your problem resolved?"

She took a deep breath and massaged her trembling hands. "Yeah, more or less. Tina agreed to let me go, but called it an unauthorized absence. I gather that's one step better than a 'no-call-no-show.' I have no idea. These clowns make up the rules as they go along."

Nora arrived, pulled out two chairs facing each other and sat, using the second as a footrest. Her feet looked like sausages, and her ankles were swollen to twice their normal size.

"What the fuck is this all about? Some kind of half-assed mandatory memorial service for the bitch? Must be—it's the only way anybody would attend," Nora snapped.

"I find such derogatory remarks about our late shift manager highly offensive. Tina was a compassionate woman and a whiz at her job. I was very fond of her," Ralph said, taking a seat without asking and glaring at Nora with his eyes narrowed.

Nora glared back at him. "Tina was an incompetent asshole and if you don't move by the time I count to three, I'm going to crawl across this table, wrap my fingers around your fat neck, and squeeze until your beady little eyes pop out. One…"

Ralph moved to another table. Cassie, Greg, and I laughed.

"Who found Janet?" I asked.

Greg shrugged. "I heard one of the housekeeping staff came in to empty wastebaskets and found her on the floor."

Most of the seats were now taken and the remaining shift personnel filed in. Several people laid their heads on the tables and dozed. Greg sat with his arms crossed over his chest, his chin down, and his eyes closed. I doubted if he slept, but his posture indicated he didn't want to chat either. Nora spoke with a couple of boxmen from the craps pit who sat with us. Cassie and I discussed her trip to California. Spivey and the cops kept us waiting another forty-five minutes before finally making an appearance.

Spivey walked past Greg and paused to whisper something in his ear. Greg nodded and glared.

The casino manager and several uniformed policemen stood at the front of the room. Howard Spivey carried a good amount of weight on a medium frame. On the wrong side of fifty, his thinning brown hair was liberally sprinkled with gray as was his Adolf Hitler style moustache. It looked silly, but apropos. However, nothing about old Howard shouted that *he* was in control of anything.

"Ladies and gentlemen, I don't think I need to tell you that Tina Rosetti has passed away. Her death is both a professional and personal loss to us. We'll all miss her."

"Yeah, like a rash on my ass," Cassie said sotto voice. One of the boxmen overheard and grinned.

"I also have the unfortunate duty to tell you that my secretary, Janet Washington, has also died."

Murmurs and shocked gasps rose from some in the crowd.

"This is Remington Wilcox, the Terence County Sheriff," he continued with a nod to the tall man standing next to him. "He has a few words to say. Sheriff."

Wilcox stepped forward, his chocolate brown face set in stern lines. His penetrating gaze swept the room. No one moved. The silence was total. Here was a man in command.

Finally, he spoke. "Ladies and gentlemen, we are currently reviewing the surveillance tapes from this evening. We also have a list of people who received reprimands in the last week, including tonight. When I call your name, please identify yourself."

He took out a slip of paper and called out the names.

"Dallas Daniels."

"Here."

"Gregory Holland."

Greg raised his hand, but said nothing.

"Anne Sherman."

"That's me," Anne replied in a small shaky voice.

He nodded and continued calling names. Another policeman entered the room with a second sheet of paper and handed it to the sheriff.

"We've finished reviewing the tapes. In addition to

the names already called, I need these people to identify themselves. Cassandra Severin."

"Yo," Cassie said, raising her hand.

"Nora Nelson." No answer. "Nora Nelson," he repeated in a louder voice.

"I'm here, goddamn it. Can we get on with this?" She placed a hand on her bulging belly. "This kid craves sleep. He's doing jumping jacks."

He rattled off another dozen names ending with, "Ralph Klinger."

Ralph the Rat raised his hand and protested. "But I was asked to come in by Tina. She gave me an attaboy."

I groaned. That figured. An "attaboy" was the opposite of a write-up. The yellow slips denoted a job well done. Ralph could probably paper his bathroom in *yellow* as opposed to my pink.

Sheriff Wilcox ignored him. "Those of you whose names were not called may leave. The rest stay put."

Most of the personnel left. About twenty-five of us stayed.

"Everyone take a seat," the sheriff said when the room was quiet.

Cliff took one of the vacated chairs at our table. His lips twitched in an effort to smile. He reminded me of a frightened rabbit.

"You are about to be questioned and are all considered suspects in the murders of Tina Rosetti and Janet Washington."

Chapter Four

The silence greeting the sheriff's announcement was thicker than my mother's gravy. Several people gasped. I don't know why they were surprised. We'd all been herded into the conference room for a purpose, and what other purpose would that be but murder?

A quick glance around our table showed varying expressions. Greg cocked an eyebrow. Anne's eyes filled with tears and she covered her mouth with a trembling hand. Cassie heaved a sigh and crossed her arms over her chest, while muttering something unintelligible. Nora didn't look any in the least surprised, and as usual, didn't keep her feelings to herself.

She snorted. "I can see someone offing Tina, but why Janet?"

The sheriff stared at her. "I take it you didn't like the late Mrs. Rosetti?"

"She was incompetent and owed her job to family connections."

Ralph cleared his throat and frowned. "I found Tina to be an exceptional shift manager. She was fair and tried to work with those who didn't have as much experience as she did."

Nora curled her lip. "Suck up."

Howard Spivey glared. "Ralph is right. Tina fulfilled her duties to my satisfaction."

"That figures. No wonder this place is such a dump. You assholes, she worked with people more experienced to suck their brains dry."

"I am tired of the negative comments expressed by employees regarding this casino. They destroy morale," Howard snapped.

Nora ignored him and shifted in her seat. "Can we get on with this? I feel like shit."

Spivey glared at Nora again, but said nothing.

Sheriff Wilcox regained control of the discussion. "In that case, let's begin with you, Mrs…?"

"Nelson, Nora Nelson."

"And your position?"

"I'm a dual-rate pit manager."

"Mrs. Nelson, I know little about the inner workings of the casino business. What's a dual-rate pit manager?"

"A dual-rate is someone who is in training for a job. In my case, a pit manager position. I floor a couple of nights a week and either manage a pit or run relief for pit managers the rest of the time."

"I see. If you don't mind, I'll set up a table over there for my questions. Please follow me."

He strode to a vacated table on the opposite side of the room. Nora heaved her swollen body upright muttering something that sounded like "officious bastard," and then waddled after him. Spivey jerked his head at Ralph who rose, and followed the big boss. They finally paused by the serving tables where Spivey talked and the rat listened. Cassie spoke with Anne.

I leaned toward Greg. "I wonder how Tina was killed."

He shrugged. "You and Nora saw more than I did.

What happened?"

"She paraded around the craps pit like cock of the walk, grabbed her chest, and dropped like a stone. I thought she had a heart attack."

Greg looked at me for the first time since entering the conference room. "Did she have her usual cup of coffee?"

I nodded.

"Could have been poison."

"Poison? But how?"

"Why do you think we're sitting here, Dallas? All of us were in the office at one time or another tonight. An unattended mug, a flick of the wrist, and a couple of drops of cyanide would do the trick."

"Cyanide? Who the hell carries cyanide around with them, or any poison for that matter?"

"A murderer?"

"But that means it would have been planned. And how did Janet get a hold of it?"

His eyebrows drew together as he frowned. "How the hell should I know? Do I look like a cop?"

His voice had a sharp quality as though he was worried.

Greg had been my first champion when I applied for the dual-rate floor supervisor position. He taught me a lot about floor duties and was patient with my mistakes—of which there were many. He was compassionate and totally professional, which helped given our past relationship.

His dry sense of humor and ability to cut through the corporate bullshit endeared him to a lot of dealers and floors, including me. Maybe a little too much. It didn't endear him to management. Greg knew how a pit, and more importantly, how a casino should be run. Believe me, the Casablanca wasn't it.

What had always struck me the most was that no matter how busy or harassed, he took the time to answer questions about the job at hand and wanted us to succeed. He'd been there, done that, and hadn't forgotten.

However, over the last couple of months I'd noticed a change. Greg laughed less and his comments often contained a trace of bitterness toward management and the business in general. And tonight, he'd looked angry enough to kill.

I leaned in closer and lowered my voice. "What went down between you and Tina tonight?"

"The usual. She wrote me up again saying my future with this casino was in doubt."

"She always said that. Why was this any different?"

His lips thinned into a harsh line, and his gray eyes darkened. For the first time, I noticed the threads of gray streaking his light brown hair. I couldn't call him good-looking in the sense of drop dead gorgeous, but I'd always felt comfortable around him—a comfort that was re-developing into a whole lot more. No matter how hard I tried, those three months stood out in my mind like a lighthouse beacon in the fog. Moving on was impossible as long as I clung to the memories. Yet I clutched for them at every opportunity. Did that make me pathetic? Probably, but I couldn't help it.

"Greg," I prompted at his silence.

"Look, Dallas, we got into an argument, okay? We called each other a few names, and I said if Tina didn't watch it someone would plant her in the nearest cotton field or toss her body into the river."

"Oh, my God, that sounds like a threat. Did anyone else overhear it?"

He ran a hand through his hair. A worried expression crept into his eyes. "The door was closed, but Janet was at her desk in the reception room, and Spivey was in his office."

"Those doors have the consistency of cardboard."

Greg rested his elbows on the table and buried his face in his hands.

"What aren't you telling me?"

He raised his head and looked into my eyes. "Spivey must have heard our raised voices and came in asking what was going down. He agreed with Tina. That's when it got heated. I was told to report to Spivey's office after shift. I think he had every intention of firing me."

Before I could comment, Nora duck-walked back to the table, her face a mask of anger.

"Sonofabitchin' cop won't let me go home. I'll be damned if I sit on these hard assed chairs any longer. Where's Spivey? I'm gonna use the sofa in his office."

I glanced toward where I'd last seen him. Ralph now sat by himself on a chair in the corner with his shoulders slumped. He wiped his eyes on his sleeve. He must have really been taking Tina's death hard. Howard was nowhere in sight.

Nora didn't wait for an answer, but swayed out of the room. I wondered how, with her abusive attitude, she kept her job. I speculated the dirt she had on Howard and Tina must have been higher than Mount Everest.

My attention snapped back to the front of the room

when the sheriff called out, "Gregory Holland, it's your turn."

Greg said nothing, but rose and walked toward the table. Cassie broke off her conversation with the pit clerk.

"So, who do you think did it?" she asked.

"I have no idea, but the list of suspects is long and distinguished. Have *you* ever seen anyone die in a casino before?"

"Kinda. I was flooring on a riverboat in Central Illinois. The thing was packed on the weekends. This player had hit a losing streak. He got up telling the dealer he'd be right back. A few minutes later this big commotion sounded from the deck below. Seems the player had decided to commit suicide by jumping into the river, only the upper deck was not as wide as the lower deck, so he missed and landed on steel. Broke both his legs. I told the dealer the guy wouldn't be returning, but he had already placed the checks the dude had behind the discard box. When I asked why, he said he'd seen the player plummet past the window."

"Oh my God, you've got to be kidding!" I didn't know whether to laugh or be horrified.

"Nope, swear on a stack of Bibles, it's the truth."

Cassie wiped a line of sweat from her forehead, and I didn't like her pasty color.

"Are you all right?"

"Yeah, I told you two-hour rotations make me sick. I'll be better once I get some sleep. Is there any water around?"

I glanced back at the buffet tables. "I see some pitchers and glasses. Sit still, I'll get it."

The ice had long since melted, but I poured a

couple of glasses anyway. The restaurant staff hadn't finished the cleanup. Unused plates, coffee cups, and utensils from steak knives to shrimp forks sat off to one side.

I yawned. It was a shame no coffee or rolls remained. I was tired and hungry. Cassie looked like she could use a bite to eat, too.

"Here. It's not cold, but it's wet," I told her when I returned.

"Thanks." She drank half of it before coming up for air. "Much better."

"Would you like an aspirin?"

"No, I don't do pills. Get 'em stuck in my throat every time." She gazed toward the sheriff's table. "I hope they take me next, so I can go home."

"They told Nora to stick around."

"Bet that made her day. It's hard to tell who's the bigger bitch—Tina or Nora."

I noted Anne now sat at the table next to us talking with the craps pit clerk.

"Why are they keeping Anne? I know she got a write-up yesterday, but was she in the office, too?"

"Said she went in on her first break wanting an apology from Tina. It seems Tina had called her incompetent and a moron. Anne took exception to it."

"And she's just now getting around to complaining?"

Cassie shrugged. "You know Annie—very quiet and reserved. She likes to think things over before acting."

"We should all have such an attitude. Tell me, what is it about this business that sends perfectly average women into total bitch mode?" I shook my head and gulped half the lukewarm water.

"Until the last few years, we found it hard to advance any higher than dealer. When I broke into the business, all the floors and pits were men. Same in Atlantic City. Then other states discovered how much money gambling generated. New casinos had no choice but to promote us. There weren't that many qualified men to go around. I left Reno for a riverboat in East St. Louis, Illinois. I imagine the same goes for Nora."

"So, it was be a bitch or deal for the rest of your life?"

"Yeah, but in Nora's case I don't think she had to work too hard at being a bitch. Maybe she killed Tina just because she felt like it."

"I wouldn't put it past her, especially now. She's due to go on maternity leave in a few weeks." I took another sip of water as Cassie finished hers. "Greg thinks someone slipped poison into Tina's coffee mug."

"That sounds as reasonable an explanation as any. My preferred method would be to blow her brains out."

"Naw, too loud. How about stabbing her in the office, and then waiting for someone else to find the body?"

"Too messy. You're bound to get blood on your clothes. How would you explain that?"

Anne rejoined us. "What are you talking about?"

"How we'd have killed Tina. What did Sherry have to say?" I referred to the craps pit clerk. "She had a ringside seat. What happened?"

"She said Tina came into the pit and kibitzed on the games as usual. She complained about an upset stomach ten or fifteen minutes later and claimed everything looked blurred. Then Sherry told me she said something like, 'I don't feel so hot. I think I'm gonna barf, and my heart's racing a million miles an hour. Maybe I should go to the infirmary.' A few seconds later, she made a funny noise, grabbed her chest, and keeled over." Anne shuddered. "She whacked her head on the Sherry's desk. Said it sounded like a gunshot."

"Sounds like a heart attack to me," Cassie said.

"Yeah, but explain Janet."

"We don't even know how she died. Maybe it's the night for heart attacks," Anne said.

Two fatal heart attacks within minutes of each other sounded too coincidental to me. Must have been on Sheriff Wilcox's mind, too.

I finished my water when Greg returned and took his seat. "Well?" I asked.

"I've been told to stick around. I have the feeling anyone who went into that office tonight will be bench warming for a while."

"Yeah, well if they expect me to sit around much longer, they'd better provide a cot because I'm exhausted," Cassie muttered. She blotted sweat from her hairline with a napkin. Her hands shook.

The sheriff called out the name of another employee. A boxman rose, sauntered over to the table, and sat.

I turned my attention to Anne. Short and on the plump side, her sweet disposition was a winner with most pit personnel. "Cassie said you're on the hot seat because you wanted an apology. Did you get it?"

The pit clerk shook her head. "I didn't ask."

"Why not?"

She shifted on her chair. "It was kind of

embarrassing."

"What was embarrassing?" Cassie wanted to know.

"I overheard something I wasn't supposed to and rather than wait around, I left. I told Janet I'd be back later."

Greg gazed at her with a frown. "What did you overhear?"

Anne looked around, and then said in a low voice, "I heard Howard and Tina yelling at Ralph in Howard's office."

"Yelling? What about? He just said he got another attaboy. What did the great suck-up do?" Now, this was news to appreciate. I couldn't wait to discover how Mr. Perfect had screwed up.

Anne looked around again and lowered her voice even further. "Well, the door wasn't closed all the way, so I heard Tina say Ralph was useless to her now, and Howard told him he—meaning Ralph—was an idiot to let himself be had by the guys. Ralph got all defensive and said he was loyal and only doing the right thing. Howard called him an asshole, and told Ralph to come back to the office after shift. Then Ralph said something like, 'You can't do this to me,' and I swear to God, I thought I heard him crying. That's when I left."

"Oh, I'd have loved to see Ralph the Rat in tears over a reprimand," I crowed. "What was Janet's reaction?"

"She was just as embarrassed as me."

"What did Howard mean by Ralph being had?" Cassie asked.

Greg chuckled. "I know the answer to that."

Before he could tell us, the sheriff called another

name and a dealer from Pit One came forward. The previous interviewee left presumably released to go home.

"Okay, Holland, spill it," I said. "What happened to Ralph?"

"Two floors in the craps pit had had it with Ralph and his eavesdropping, so they set him up a couple of days ago just before shift started and the dealers arrived."

"How?" Anne asked.

"They pretended to check the count on one of the closed tables. Ralph was loitering right behind them."

"Of course, he was," I commented, loving this.

"So, they talked in voices low enough to sound conspiratorial, but loud enough for Ralph to hear, about how the count is off by ten grand and somebody's head will be decorating Howard's wall."

Cassie laughed. "Let me guess, Ralph ran to Tina and told her *he* discovered the error."

Greg formed his index finger and thumb into a gun and pointed at her. "You got it. Tina came flying out of the office demanding to know why a table count was off by ten thousand dollars. I heard the guys who pulled the trick laughed their asses off at both of them, and then bought write-ups for conduct unbecoming a floor supervisor or some such bullshit."

"I'd take a write-up for that," Cassie said.

"How come they just got around to reaming him out tonight?" I wondered.

"Howard was off the last two days," Greg said.

"Anne Sherman, please come forward," the sheriff called.

Anne jumped. "Oh, dear, what do I tell them? Do I

mention Ralph?"

"Damned straight you do," Cassie said. "He has a motive and that makes him a suspect."

"Anne Sherman," Sheriff Wilcox repeated in a louder voice.

"Here! I mean, I'm coming," Anne said, trotting away.

"Do you believe this shit?" Yolanda Harris said plopping her more than ample ass in Anne's vacated chair.

Yolanda needed no description. She stood close to five-feet-nine-inches tall and her figure reminded me of an enormous well-packed snowman. The first time I ever met her she wore a bubblegum pink, strapless, spandex mini-dress at least two sizes too small and combat boots. She had a voice like brass and wasn't afraid to use it. If you talked about Yolanda, no one ever said, "Yolanda Who?"

She had also recently been canned from her day shift cashier's job at the casino.

"Yolanda, what are you doing here? I thought you got fired?" I asked.

"I did. Anything to drink in this dump?"

"Water on the back table," Cassie said. "Why'd you buy the unemployment line?"

"Water? Crap, I want a beer."

"Why were you fired?" Cassie repeated.

"Huh? Oh, some drunk accused me of shorting him. He called me a couple of names and I told him where to shove it. He tried to crawl through the cage window and across the counter, so I whacked him up alongside the head with my fist. Security came and busted it up. Pretty good fight, if you ask me. At any rate, a few days later I get called into the office. That asshole Spivey waves a letter under my nose from some lawyer saying that if I'm not fired, his client will sue. So, guess what? I got canned."

I suspected that was only part of the reason. Yolanda's foul mouth and nasty attitude supplied the remainder.

"But why are you here with the rest of us?" Greg asked.

"I came in late this afternoon to sign my formal separation papers. Around seven I popped into Spivey's office to tell him what I thought of him. Security escorted me from the premises. So, I went to the Golden Hoard for a while, and then sneaked back in here through the employee entrance and played at BJ 4 over in Pit One." She defied the "No Smoking" signs and lit up. "By one-thirty or so, I was broke and had enough beer in me to take another shot at Spivey."

"What did you call him this time around?" Cassie asked.

"Never talked to him. I listened. No one was in the outer office—guess Janet must have been on a break. At any rate he was in Tina's office. The door wasn't closed and I heard everything."

"This must be the night for eavesdropping. What'd you hear?" I said.

"Howard was demanding Tina break off her relationship with—get this—that miserable piece of shit, Ralph Klinger."

"Tina—and Ralph?" Cassie's eyebrows rose almost to her hairline. "You've got to be kidding. Just the thought of boinking Ralph is enough to make me hurl."

"But it kept Ralph under control," Greg said. "Tina was incompetent, not stupid. String him along with a bunch of attaboys, keep him off balance with a little sex on the side, and she wouldn't have to promote him beyond floor supervisor. He'd repeat every snippet of information overheard. Then when his usefulness is over—like now—she dumps him."

"Holy shit! Talk about a motive," I murmured. "What was Tina's response to Howard's demand?"

Yolanda blew out a noxious stream of smoke. I waved my hand in what was for me a subtle suggestion. She ignored it. Subtlety was lost on the woman.

"Said it was already in the works, and they both laughed. Then I heard a bunch of sounds that can only be described as affectionate and beat it."

"Wait a minute, Tina was also doing Howard?" Cassie said. "You know, this is probably the most morally corrupt casino I've ever worked in, and that includes Reno."

A security man tapped Yolanda on the shoulder. "Ma'am, there's no smoking in this room."

"Yeah, yeah, whatever," she muttered, dumping the cigarette in Cassie's glass. The glowing tip hissed in the remaining water.

Anne returned. "I have to stay, too. I think anyone who's on that tape after shift started is on the hit list."

"Yolanda Harris."

"About fucking time." She rose, rearranged her long blonde hair in the banana clip holding it on top of her head, pulled the fuchsia spandex crop pants out of her ass, and then strutted on four-inch high heels to the sheriff's table.

Time dragged. Anne drifted back over to talk with

Sherry. Cassie used her arms as a pillow on the table. Greg sat with his feet outstretched, ankles crossed, arms folded, his chin resting on his chest, and dozed.

I was too wound up to sleep. The clock on the wall read five-thirty. My stomach grumbled and I wondered if management would think to send any food in our direction. Probably not. Cheap bastards.

Yolanda left the sheriff's table and stomped to the nearest phone. She punched in a couple of numbers and waited. Then her voice blared like a klaxon through the room.

"Spivey, quit treating us like cattle and get some goddamned food and coffee up here. This questioning shit is taking forever...Yeah, this is Yolanda, and if you want me talk nice about you when it's my turn, you'll feed us now."

She slammed the receiver back down, pulled a pack of Marlboros from her purse, and lit up. A security guard approached. She pointed the burning end at him like a sword.

"Back off, buster. I don't give a damn about any fucking signs. If I have to stay here, I want my comfort. Go find me an ashtray."

The man stared at the glaring two hundred-fifty pound woman, turned, grabbed a plate from the buffet, and handed it to her. She slapped it on the nearest table, and then straddling a chair, kept her gaze focused on the doors, no doubt awaiting the arrival of sustenance.

"Ten bucks says Spivey delivers in fifteen minutes," Greg said without opening his eyes.

"Less," Cassie murmured. "Breakfast is being served in the Blue Parrot Buffet. He's probably scrounging for dinner leftovers in the kitchen."

I rested my elbow on the table, propped my chin in my hand, and watched the proceedings with half-closed eyes. The sheriff called out names on a regular basis. Most of the questioned staff left.

"Cassandra Severin."

"Finally, although I don't expect to be going anywhere."

Cassie walked over with shoulders slumped. Her interview took fifteen minutes, during which the food arrived. Surprisingly, it wasn't leftovers, but a full breakfast array of scrambled eggs, bacon and sausage, fruit, biscuits, and coffee. Spivey must have grabbed the first chafing dishes out of the kitchen. I wondered if he actually thought Yolanda would give him a kind word.

Greg and I along with a dozen other people filled plates and cups. I shoveled food into my mouth like I would never see another meal.

Cassie was finally released and hurried to the buffet. Another name was called.

"God, I am so tired," she said setting her plate on the table.

Her skin was even paler than before, and as she lifted a coffee cup to her lips, her hand shook spilling some of the liquid.

"Are you sure you're all right?"

She nodded. "Yeah, yeah. I just don't feel well. Maybe food will help. How much longer can they keep us here?"

"If the sheriff's smart, he'll have already sent blood samples from both victims to Memphis. They have more forensic resources than down here," Greg told her. "I wouldn't be surprised to find out the autopsies are also taking place immediately."

"I thought it took a while to get results from blood," I said munching on a slice of bacon.

"The Med has most of the bells and whistles needed to determine alcohol levels and simple toxins." He smiled, but eyed Cassie with a worried look. "Hope he's not dragging this out until he gets the results. We could be here for days."

I polished off my biscuit and considered a refill on my coffee when the sheriff called, "Dallas Daniels."

I swallowed and my stomach clenched. I'd never been questioned by cops before and had certainly never been a suspect in a murder.

Greg squeezed my hand and smiled. "Don't worry, you'll be fine."

His soft words and the look on his face made me wonder once again how much he knew about my fantasies or my hopes and if he had any of his own. I took a deep breath.

"Yeah, I know."

I approached the Sheriff Wilcox's table, but couldn't keep the nervous flutter from making my hands tremble.

I had as good a motive as anybody. Would he arrest me?

Chapter Five

"Please, have a seat, Ms. Daniels."

I sat and stared into Sheriff Wilcox's dark eyes. My whole body trembled. He stared back for a second before smiling.

"Just relax. This isn't the third degree. Ms. Daniels, what is your job here?"

He had several sheets of paper in front of him. I figured he already knew, but answered anyway.

"I'm a floor supervisor. I worked tonight in Pit Two, area one, the end section with the roulette table."

"I see you were reprimanded this evening. Tell me about it."

I inhaled a deep breath to steady my nerves and launched into the saga of Cliff and the overpayment.

The sheriff raised his hand. "Just a minute, Miss Daniels. I don't gamble, so some of the terminology is new to me. What's a check?"

"A check is the chip used on the tables instead of money. Red is worth five dollars, green twenty-five, black a hundred, and so on."

How could he live in Terence and not know this? Or maybe he was testing my knowledge, although for what purpose I couldn't fathom. On the other hand, maybe I was just tired and suspicious.

"So, why are they called checks instead of chips?"

I shrugged. "I don't know. Maybe because they

have a fixed worth, are the same color from casino to casino, and cashable. The only *chips* in a casino are the colored discs on roulette tables. Their value is whatever the customer wants down to table minimum."

"I see." He smiled. I could have sworn he meant it. "Now, tell me what you saw this evening in the craps pit."

I kept my answer to a bare minimum and gave him what I'd seen, not what Nora, Greg, and I had discussed. I figured they were in trouble enough already.

"Mrs. Nelson was rather vocal in her assessment of Ms. Rosetti. Do you concur with her opinion?" he asked.

I shifted in my seat. This was trickier. Most of us had been vocal at one time or another about the management.

"I really didn't have that much contact with Tina. I'm a lowly floor supervisor. Other than a simple hello now and again, we didn't speak."

"Except, of course, when you're getting reprimanded."

I squirmed again, but didn't answer. What could I say?

"Tell me about Mr. Holland. How well do you know him?"

A lot better than you can ever imagine, both in reality and my dreams. Naturally, I didn't say that.

"He came here three years ago as a pit manager. I was a dealer then and he, along with a sympathetic floor supervisor, helped me get a promotion."

"And who would that be?" He cast a glance around the room at the remaining personnel.

"The floor? Cassie Severin. She's been in the business for a long time and knew when to make a comment on my work and when to be quiet."

"Let's see, Mr. Holland and Ms. Severin were in the office tonight. Do you know why?"

"Don't you? You've already talked to them." I couldn't keep the tart tone from my voice. A simple no would have sufficed. No diplomacy.

"Just thought maybe they'd elaborated on the experience with you, that's all."

It occurred to me that perhaps Sheriff Wilcox had asked the same question of Greg and Cassie about me.

"Cassie had a scheduling snafu that needed attention, and I don't know about Greg. He didn't say. The pit was busy tonight. Not much time for casual conversation."

The sheriff pulled a photo from a file folder by his right hand.

"Do you know these people?"

I stared at a grainy picture of Goofy and Daffy just outside the office. The time at the bottom read zero one-ten.

"Yeah, they're customers. I've floored them on several occasions. They play roulette."

"Why would they be going into the manager's office?"

I told him about the dust up regarding the laser accusation.

"Are you kidding me?" he said with raised eyebrows.

I shook my head. "Nope. They're a couple of screwballs."

"Do you know their names?"

"I think the last name is Carlson. They have players' cards, and I checked them in. It should be in the electronic files."

"How angry were they?"

"On a scale of one to ten, I'd say a solid eight. I kind of laughed at them."

"What would the shift manager have to say to them?"

"I have no idea, but not even Tina would have given them the time of day. She'd have taken their complaint and that would have been the end of it." At least, I hoped that's what had happened.

"We found a note scribbled on a slip of paper on her desk. It said, 'Talk to Dallas about customer relations.'" He smiled again.

I detected a predatory gleam in his eyes. Swell, if Tina hadn't dropped dead, I'd have been on the hot seat for a second time after shift.

"Nobody said anything to me about it." I tried to keep my voice casual and disinterested.

He replaced the photo and handed me another. "And this person?"

"Yolanda Harris. You talked to her, too."

"She was fired earlier in the week. Had an argument with Mr. Spivey around seven in the evening and was escorted from the premises. As you can see, she reentered the office at one-forty-two. Talk to her tonight?"

"Just here."

"She say anything of interest?"

"Yolanda says a lot, most of it aggressive and often profane not to mention blasphemous."

The sheriff took the photo from my fingers and

replaced it in the file.

"Thank you for your help, Miss Daniels. Please remain in the room for a few more minutes."

I rose and walked back to the table. Cassie had finished her food and sat nursing a cup of coffee. Greg was across the room talking with Ralph, of all people. Yolanda shoveled biscuits and sausage gravy into her mouth, washing it down with a beer. God only knew where she'd gotten it. Anne stared at me with wide eyes, and then leaned forward.

"I did it. I told the sheriff about Ralph," she said.

Before any of us could answer, the sheriff called out Ralph's name. He broke off his conversation with Greg and scurried to the interrogation table. Greg sauntered over to the buffet and filled a cup from the coffee urn.

I rose and headed for the food again. Being questioned by the cops increased my appetite. Sheer nerves, I guessed.

Greg stopped me on his way back to the table. "How did it go?"

"Not as horrible as I thought. How about you?"

"Could have been worse." He smiled, his eyes focused on my mouth. "Like I said, don't worry. Nobody suspects you."

He headed back to the table, his words and expression leaving me a trifle breathless. I snatched a plate from the stack, and then turned to survey the occupants of the room. I hadn't seen Yolanda in the casino, but the photo clearly showed her entering the office about twenty minutes before Tina had come out. I'd seen Cassie heading in that direction earlier, but had no idea of the time. I knew Greg's visit had taken place sometime after my second break, which put it around midnight. Nora had also been called in for her chat near that time—or was it later? I couldn't remember. All I knew was that at about two-thirty Tina had bitten the big one.

I turned back to the buffet, filled my plate, and returned to the table. As I resumed my seat, it occurred to me that one of my friends might very well be a killer.

Greg? God knows he was angry enough, and even though I was hot for the guy, couldn't see him offing anyone. Cassie? She had a temper for sure. Nora? She didn't strike me as a poison type of person. She'd just meet you in the parking lot and beat the crap out of you. Yolanda? I could see her and Nora as a tag team, first one and then the other pounding Tina into jelly. Anne? Sweet, passive Anne? Sometimes those quiet ones were the most violent. But Anne? I didn't see it. Ralph the Rat? He was sneaky, but wouldn't have the guts.

And there was still the question of why kill Janet Washington? Had she seen something? Maybe her death was an accident. Had someone tampered with Tina's coffee and Janet got a hold of it by mistake? If so, then the contents of the coffee pot in the office became the likely source.

I raised my cup to my lips, and then put it down. Suddenly, coffee didn't seem like such a good idea. I drank from the glass of water instead.

"Oh God, when are they going to let us go?" Cassie murmured with a moan. "I have to get some sleep."

The food didn't appear to have helped. She looked awful.

"Hey, at least I'm getting free food out of the deal," Yolanda said, talking through the food in her mouth. "Knowing Spivey, he'll take the cost out of your paychecks next week."

"Doesn't matter to me. I probably won't be here to care," Greg replied.

"You quitting or getting canned like me?"

"Definitely canned. Reserve a spot for me in the unemployment line."

"Good God, what did go on in the office tonight?" I asked.

Greg shrugged and gulped some coffee. "I popped off in the break room yesterday about the food. It's unappetizing and they charge us for the privilege of eating it. Tina called me in just before shift began and told me to knock it off. I told her this was the only casino I'd ever worked in where the employees had to pay for their food. One meal a night is usually a freebie. She claimed I was destroying morale with my negativity. I told her she was full of shit, made the comment about the cotton field, and walked out."

I chewed a slice of bacon. "That was for what happened last night. What about tonight?"

"More of the same. On my first break, I made a comment to the effect that this casino is the worst run, employee screwing, cheapest place I'd ever seen or worked in. The next thing I knew I was called out of the pit and into the office."

"Was Ralph around when you said it?" Cassie asked.

"Don't know. Probably. Tina said she'd had it with my attitude and something had to be done. Spivey came in demanding to know what was going on, so I repeated what I'd said. Howard put his two cents worth in, too. He told me we'd discuss my future at the Casablanca after shift. I saw the handwriting on the wall and let 'em have it with both barrels."

"Oh, Greg, what did you say?" Anne said, her eyes wide.

"I called them frauds, incompetent, and if they fired me, I'd be talking to the Mississippi Gaming Commission about how this casino is run."

I choked on my scrambled eggs. "You didn't!"

"I did. Spivey told me to get out. I think he may have meant the casino, not the office. At any rate, he still wants to talk to me tomorrow evening before shift."

"You're a goner," Yolanda said, draining her beer.

"Eight dollars an hour at the local discount store is looking better and better," I muttered.

"Amen," Cassie said with a yawn. "When the hell are we going to get out of here?"

As if to answer her question, the sheriff rose from the table and conferred with another officer. Ralph sat by himself at a table near the back of the room apparently having been dismissed from the interview while we'd talked. I craned my neck for a better look.

Ralph the Rat didn't look too good. His frightened face was white and his gaze darted around the room. He ran a shaking hand over his lips. I'd have given a week's salary to have heard what he and the sheriff had discussed.

"Ladies and gentlemen."

My attention shifted to Sheriff Wilcox who now stood in front of the table. My stomach clenched. Would he arrest somebody? Me? Greg? Cassie? Someone else?

"I want to thank all of you for your cooperation and patience. I know you've put in a long day and are tired. As of now you are free to go home. Just don't anybody leave the area for a few days. The casino has supplied me with your schedules. I'll be back tomorrow to talk to some of you further. Good night."

"About time," Cassie said, rising. She stumbled slightly and clutched at the back of her chair.

I grasped her upper arm. "You're not all right. Maybe you should stop by the infirmary."

"No need. I'm fine." She shook my hand off and smiled. "Just so damned tired I can hardly stand it."

Greg reached out to support her other arm. "Why don't you let me drive you home?"

She also pulled away from his hand. "No, really, I'll be fine. Thank God I live in Swansea. It's only a short drive. I'll see you tomorrow." She turned and walked through the door with a controlled gait.

"Well, I'm outta here, too." Yolanda picked up the beer bottle and tilted it to her lips to catch any lingering drops. Finding none, she made a face and tossed it onto the table with a clatter. Without another word, she, too, left.

Most of the group had gone. I hadn't seen Nora in a while, but assumed someone would relay the message to her. Knowing Nora, she'd probably gone home the minute she was out of the room.

"You still going to the Golden Hoard?" Greg asked as we walked toward the staircase.

"No way. I'm too tired. I'm heading home and hitting the sack. Tomorrow should be interesting. What else can the sheriff possibly ask us?"

"For starters, he might have the results of the blood and tox screens. Maybe even the preliminaries of the autopsies. While we've been in here, I'll bet they've been searching our lockers."

"Can they do that without a warrant?" Somehow I didn't like the idea of a stranger rooting through my stuff, including my purse. I didn't have anything to hide, but that wasn't the point.

Greg shrugged. "A crime has been committed and the lockers belong to the casino. If Spivey says it's okay, then it's okay."

"I still don't like it. It's an invasion of privacy or something."

"Got a stash hidden?" he teased.

I smacked him on the arm. "Of course not. But I'll bet there might be a couple of people who do."

"If so, they won't be here tomorrow."

All casinos were drug free, but that didn't stop a few dealers, floors, and pits from taking a drag of pot or a snort of coke every now and then, usually out in the employee parking lot. Same with booze. A bottle under the seat wasn't unusual. But not even a moron kept something illegal in his locker.

We entered the break room. My locker didn't look violated, but who knew? I was sure a master key was kept somewhere by security. Opening the door, I removed my jacket and purse, and then turned. A few swing shift personnel still lingered. The graveyard workers on break didn't make eye contact with any of us. Word spread fast.

Greg waited for me in the hallway. "I'll walk you to your car."

For some reason, I was touched by his concern. I admitted I was nervous about strolling through the parking lot at dawn after a couple of murders. He cupped my elbow with warm fingers, sending an even warmer feeling surging through me. I fumbled for something to say. Out of the pit, he was no longer my pit manager and supervisor, but a friend, a man—and my former lover. Plus, there were all those fantasies and erotic dreams.

His next words took me by surprise. "How about we meet somewhere in Swansea for dinner before shift tomorrow?"

"Ah…yeah…sure…why not?" I stammered. "Any place in particular?"

"Donovan's?" he suggested naming a chain restaurant on Goodman Road known for steaks and beer.

"Sounds good to me. What time?"

"Five? I know that's early, but if we wait until later, we might not get out in time for work."

We halted next to my Toyota Corolla. I cleared my throat and gazed into his gray eyes. Why was this so awkward? I'd known him for several years, had slept with him. Now after almost three years of determined professional behavior, he'd just asked me out on a date.

"That makes sense."

He smiled, leaned down and brushed his lips over my forehead.

My knees almost buckled. I nodded silently, forced myself to relax, unlocked my car, and opening the door, slid behind the wheel.

"I'll see you tomorrow at five." He closed the door, waved, and turned toward his car further up the row. He didn't apologize for the semi-kiss either, which sent a rush of sheer happiness through me.

I stared, my mind conjuring up a romantic, candlelit dinner with great food and fine wine. Maybe those erotic dreams would come true again after all. Then reality splashed me in the face with a bucket of cold water. *Get a grip, Daniels.*

I pushed prurient thoughts into the back of my mind, started my car and backed out of the space. As I sped away from the casino property, I wondered what the tox and blood screens would show.

By this time tomorrow, one of my friends might be charged with murder. I hoped it wasn't Greg.

Chapter Six

I pulled into a space in the parking lot at Donovan's a few minutes before five. Using the rearview mirror, I checked my hair and make-up before deciding there wasn't enough concealer in the country to hide the dark circles under my eyes. I made a face, twisted the mirror back into place, and exited.

The lowering sun set the western sky ablaze in a red-orange glow. Toward the southwest, a darkening on the horizon suggested storm clouds brewing. I hoped nothing worse than a good thunderstorm was on the menu. A lifetime of living in the Mid-South made late April a time to sky watch, and I wondered if any kind of *really* bad weather was on the way.

I entered the restaurant and paused looking around for Greg, finally spotting him at the bar. A glass of red wine sat in front of him.

"Hi, am I late?"

He gazed at me with a smile and patted the stool next to him. He looked as if sleep had been elusive.

"Not as far as I know."

"You don't look so hot."

"Didn't sleep well."

I hadn't either. I was awake too often to enjoy any dreams of Greg.

He signaled the bartender. "Name your poison."

"Greg, that's not funny!"

He took a deep breath. "No, I guess it's not. Sorry. What would you like to drink?"

I'm not fond of drinking before shift. Booze makes me sleepy after a while and being responsible for all that casino money didn't mix with drowsiness. On the other hand, I still had three hours to work it off.

"Red wine will do."

Greg placed my order and picking up his glass, slid off the stool. "Let's get a table."

Due to the early hour, we had our choice of seating and selected a booth on the other side of the bar area.

For some reason I was nervous. I didn't know if it was being alone with Greg after so much time had passed or our connection to what had transpired the night before. Greg was also silent. Not that he was any kind of garrulous type of guy. In the pit, he was all business—except when massaging my neck, that is—but in the break room his pithy sense of humor often came through. It was part of his attraction. I hadn't seen much of it when we'd been dating, but now found it an integral piece of his personality. I wondered if he understood how much I liked being near him. I had learned to live with platonic. Now, I wanted more.

A waitress brought my drink and handed us menus.

"Give us few minutes," he told her.

She nodded and left. I sipped the wine allowing the full-bodied Cabernet to slide down my throat. For a house variety, it wasn't bad.

"So, did you get much sleep, Dallas?"

"No. I kept dreaming all the patrons in the casino died and I was the only one left standing."

"I didn't sleep so good either. Too much on my mind." He sipped, his gaze never wavering from my face.

"Who do you think did it?"

"Haven't got a clue and don't really care. The bitch is dead and off my back. And don't frown at me like that. You can't be terribly sorry she's gone either."

"I may not have liked Tina, but no one deserves to be murdered," I said taking another sip.

"I don't know, I can think of several people I wouldn't mind offing."

"Including Janet? Why kill her?"

His expression softened. "It's too bad about her. She was a nice lady, but in the military, she'd be referred to as collateral damage."

"In the wrong place at the wrong time?"

He shrugged. "A by-product of the main mission."

"Killing Tina." I inhaled a shaky breath. "Have you ever heard of someone being murdered in a casino—an employee, I mean?"

He frowned and shook his head. "Not that I can remember, and I started in this business in Atlantic City twenty years ago."

"I thought about this most of the day. Someone did it, but I can't figure out who. I mean, I just can't see one of my friends or acquaintances waltzing into the office and poisoning Tina."

"We don't know for sure it was poison," he cautioned.

"What else?" I sipped more wine. What else, indeed?

"Heart attack?"

"And Janet? Did she just happen to have a heart attack an hour or so later, too?"

Greg drew in a deep breath and let it out again in a

rush. "Okay, you win. It was poison. I never really suspected otherwise. And judging from the list of employees who paraded into the office, the police have their work cut out for them."

The waitress returned. I hadn't even opened the menu, but did so now. Even though a steakhouse, other choices were plentiful. I finally decided on a small filet, medium rare, a baked potato, and a salad. Greg ordered the same.

"What did Sheriff Wilcox ask you?" he said when the girl had gone.

"Why had I been written up, was I angry, did I know who'd want to kill Tina? I didn't answer that one."

"Did he ask about other people in the pit?"

"Just you. I said you hadn't told me why you'd been called into the office. Then he showed me a couple of surveillance photos—one of Yolanda and one of Goofy and Daffy. The last two lodged a formal complaint against me."

"Probably lodged one against me, too," he said shaking his head. "If they were going to kill someone, it would be one of us."

"Unless someone had to pick Tina up off the floor when she finished laughing. And Yolanda wouldn't use poison. Much too subtle. She's a more hands on type of person. She'd beat the shit out of Tina and leave her body wherever it fell. Same with Nora."

Greg shook his head. "Nora talks a good game, but she's not physical. She uses words to intimidate."

"She's good at it." I wasn't sure about her not getting physical, especially with her hormones out of whack and dealing with an uncomfortable pregnancy.

"What did the police ask you?"

"Pretty much the same. I downplayed the argument. No sense in having them know I suspected I was about to get canned."

"So, you figure this is like your Last Supper?"

Greg grinned. "Don't think so. I got a call from Howard a while ago. Told me our discussion about my future with the casino was on hold until the sheriff finds out who killed Tina and Janet."

I sipped more of my wine. Thank goodness. I'd miss him and our chats in the break room before shift and during whatever breaks we had together. Some nights, they were the highlight of my day. I didn't want to think of my life without Greg Holland in it.

"Who's taking over for Tina?" I asked.

"I would imagine Jack Mathias."

Jack Mathias was the assistant shift manager. He assumed those duties on Tuesday and Wednesday, Tina's days off. On the remaining nights he dropped back to pit manager. He'd been around in Vegas as a dealer and later a floor supervisor during the tumultuous '80s, once bragging at having known the real people depicted in the movie *Casino*. He wasn't the brightest bulb in the chandelier, but knew the business. Rumor had it a permanent shift manager position was his goal until retirement only a few short years away.

I liked Jack. He was a nice guy, and I worked well with him whenever he pitted me. Then a thought occurred.

"Greg, where was Jack last night? I don't remember seeing him at all."

"He was at the pre-shift pit managers' meeting. I think he was assigned to Pit Four, but you're right. He was nowhere to be found after the deaths. I remember seeing him in the break room, but not when."

"I never paid any attention to who was in Pit Four." I paused as I remembered a snippet of conversation. "Nora said something about Karl Hamilton taking over pits three and four while you were in the office. And I know Mark Davis was in the craps pit. She was pit relief last night. She'd know."

"If you ask me, Nora knows a lot."

I had to ask a question that had piqued my curiosity last night. "Greg, what on earth were you and Ralph talking about last night?"

He gave me a blank stare. "Ralph? When?"

"It was during the interviews with the sheriff. The two of you were standing near the buffet. Looked intense."

"Oh, yeah. No big deal. He was just worried about why anyone would think he'd killed Tina. Apparently, he had to explain what Anne had overheard." He sipped more wine and dropped his gaze to the table.

He was being evasive. "Given what Anne and Yolanda had to say, how could he not be considered a suspect?"

Greg shrugged. "He made it clear that in his opinion, I topped the list. Yolanda claimed second place with Nora running a close third. Don't worry about it. He was just blowing off steam."

But I did worry about it. Ralph was sneaky, and sneaky often translated into vindictive.

Our food arrived and I dug in. A good meal meant I didn't have to eat the usually crappy food at the employee cafeteria in the casino. The steak was slightly overdone and the potato underdone, but I ate it anyway.

The salad was a salad. Who screwed up lettuce and tomatoes?

We didn't say much during the meal. Time was our enemy. Greg had a meeting with the rest of the pit managers, Jack, and I assumed Howard, at seven. It was almost six and the casino was a thirty minute drive south.

The waitress brought the check and while Greg paid, I finished my wine.

"You ready?" he asked when done.

"Yeah." I slid from the booth and headed for the front door.

Greg rested his hand in the small of my back. A shiver crawled up my spine and a delicious glow settled in the pit of my stomach. Memories of those long nights making love resurfaced. Desire throbbed deep inside me. Were those fantasies about to become the real deal again?

Outside, the gathering clouds had increased adding to the tension within. Stillness hung in the air. It would storm before the night was over. I just hoped it didn't arrive while I was driving.

Greg walked me to my car, and then paused. "Uh, Dallas, it might be better if you didn't mention we had dinner or talked about the murders."

"Why not?"

"It could be misconstrued by some people. Like we were getting our stories straight."

"What?"

"And if I were you, I wouldn't ask too many questions or discuss the murders too much. We can testify to each other's whereabouts at the time Tina died. Why rock the boat? Just do your job and let the cops do theirs."

God Almighty! Was he suggesting he needed an alibi? Or did he think I needed one?

He leaned over and kissed me lightly. "Be careful driving. I'll see you in the pit."

He walked away as I slid behind the wheel. I sat still for a moment, biting my lower lip and trying to ignore the heat the kiss had generated. I almost succeeded. Had this whole dinner thing been a set up to buy my cooperation or collaboration on who'd been where when?

I could verify when he'd been in the pit, but I had no idea where he'd been while on his break. Not a clue.

The question was, how far would I go to protect him?

****

The break room was jammed and the main topic of conversation was Tina and Janet's murders. My watch read a little before seven. The day shift dealers and floor personnel mingled with those here early for swing.

I grabbed a cup of coffee to equalize the effect of the wine and found a seat next to Nora and a couple of the dual-rate boxmen.

Nora looked like hell. Most pregnant women give off a glow. But Nora just looked pregnant and like she hadn't slept in a couple of days. No amount of make-up could conceal the lines grooving her forehead or from her nose to the corners of her mouth.

She took a drink from a bottle of water and eyed me. "So, ready for another fun filled night at the Casablanca Casino and Funeral Parlor?"

One of the boxman rolled his eyes. "God, Nora.

"Do you really think I care Tina is dead?" She paused. "I am sorry about Janet. Too bad she had to go along for the ride."

For some reason I was fascinated by the subject of death in casinos. Until last night, I hadn't given it much thought. I told them Cassie's tale about the jumper on the riverboat.

"Any of you ever have a close encounter with something like that?" I asked.

Nora shrugged. "In a casino? Nope, never."

The first boxman chuckled. "I worked on a riverboat in Indiana. The captain was a lush. He was also a relative of the owner. One night, we pulled away from the dock only the sot neglected to tell anyone to cast off. The boat stopped like a running dog on the end of a leash. Anyone standing fell on their asses and those seated had to hold onto the tables to avoid hitting the floor. Tore out half the dock. Needless to say, he was canned."

We all laughed. The break room was a constant source of amusement. Much of the personnel had come from Nevada or Atlantic City. They had tales to tell. The thing was, were they tall tales or truth? Didn't matter—as long as it made me laugh.

"I got that one beat," the second man said. "I worked in Laughlin for a while. We had a dealer there who lined the roof of her car with aluminum foil."

I gulped some of my cooling coffee. "You're kidding. What the hell for?"

He leaned forward. "So the aliens wouldn't steal her thoughts. I'm serious," he said when I sputtered. "One night the floor found her dealing, conversing, and making payoffs to nobody. Her table was dead. The explanation? She was dealing to invisible aliens who promised they'd stay out of her mind if she let them win."

"Yeah, you meet all kinds in casinos," Nora commented.

As much as I enjoyed the anecdotes, my mind returned to Jack Mathias.

"Nora, you ran relief last night, was Jack in Pit Four?"

"Yeah, until I went to relieve him on the second rotation. I found Karl Hamilton taking his place."

"Wonder what happened?" I asked.

"I'd talked to Jack in the break room earlier and he said he felt like shit. Musta gone home," the one boxman replied.

"He's here tonight, which reminds me," Nora said. "I have to get to the pit meeting. I'm already late. Probably be forced to listen to a rah-rah, sis-boom-bah, let's all band together in Tina's memory bunch of bullshit." She rose. "See you later."

The boxmen wandered to another table. Outside, the dark clouds thickened and rain spattered against the windows. Lightning flashed and thunder rumbled. The storm had finally arrived.

Mira Hoskins, a day shift floor supervisor, took the vacated seat. "Geez, Dallas, what the hell happened last night? I heard someone poisoned Tina and stabbed Janet."

I jerked in surprise. "Stabbed? I didn't hear anything about her being stabbed. Where'd you get that?"

"From one of the housekeeping staff on graveyard."

The rumor mill at the Casablanca had worked overtime. I was about to dismiss the idea of a stabbing when it occurred to me no one had ever said anything about how Janet died.

"How would they know? Besides, to the best of my knowledge only pit personnel were questioned after shift."

The floor leaned in closer her eyes locked on my face and whispered, "The guy who told me said that a friend of a friend of his was called in to clean up some suspicious looking stains on the carpet. Blood you think?"

I shrugged. "Haven't heard a thing about it."

"But you were questioned, right? I heard they pulled tape and talked to everyone who went into the office. Why were you there?"

I didn't like Mira much. Arriving from Illinois, she'd been hired shortly after the casino had opened. Something about her just irritated the crap out of me.

I gave her a shortened version of last night.

"So, you got written up? Do the police think you're a suspect? Did you actually see her die?"

I'd had enough of this conversation and rose. "I doubt it, and no, I didn't see much of anything to write home about. Excuse me. I have to check my pit assignment."

I left the room and walked around the corner to the assignment board meeting several swing shift dealers arriving for work. They shook water from their raincoats and umbrellas.

"Hi, Dallas. Boy, it's really pouring out there."

I nodded but said nothing. Mira's question about Janet got me to thinking. If she was stabbed, then could

Tina's death be attributed to a heart attack? But who the hell would want to stab Janet? And why? Maybe Tina *was* poisoned and Janet killed because she could ID the killer? Made as much sense as anything else.

I shrugged and focused my attention on the bulletin board. Tonight's assignments were posted. I found my name. "Shit!"

Someone stopped next to me. "I take that to mean you are either in the P. T. Barnum Memorial Section of Pit Two or in the living hell of Pit One," Cassie said.

"Right now, I'd take all those yahoos on Caribbean Stud. I've got the roulette section of Pit One. Damn."

The front area of Pit One held four roulette games, two with varying minimums. I would also be responsible for two BJ tables, one a pitch, the other a shoe deal. Six tables. Too many for one person to watch, but that was the Casablanca for you. Squeeze your attention span until you made a mistake, and then write you up. I didn't need a second pink slip in two days. I glanced at the other pit assignments. Greg was listed to join me. At least the night wouldn't be so long with the object of my fantasies in the same pit.

"It's Sunday. By midnight the back section of the pit will close and that floor will give extra pushes for the rest of us," she said in a soothing tone.

"Where are you?" I asked Cassie.

"Where I belong, the middle section of Pit Two—probably two quarter tables and a couple of dimes. That's the good news. The bad news is Nora is my pit."

Twenty-five and ten-dollar minimum tables guaranteed a fast paced evening. With the exception of having to deal with Nora, I envied her.

"Oh well, at least Nora knows I'm competent and

doesn't hover," she said with a sigh.

"You'll still have to listen to her bitch about how uncomfortable she is. How did you sleep last night?"

Cassie looked a hundred percent improved from when I'd last seen her. Her face had some color and her eyes were clear, less tired and confused.

"Like the old proverbial baby. My head hit the pillow at six and I didn't crack an eyelid until almost four. How about you?"

"Awful. Wonder if Jack Mathias is getting the nod for shift manager."

"At least in the interim. I talked to him a while ago."

"I heard he went home last night."

She nodded. "He's on some kind of new medication and it didn't set well with him. He seems better tonight."

"What's his problem?"

She shrugged. "I can't remember. The older we get the more we need." She paused and laughed. "I talked to Spivey earlier about my vacation. He was pissed I went to HR. Said I should have tried to work it out with Tina and Charlie."

"You did and got a bunch of crap from Tina."

"And I'd rather die than try to compromise with Charlie-the-Ass-Kisser. Told Spivey that, too. He wasn't too happy, but let it go. At least for now. I'll probably get some kind of punishment when I return— if I return."

I groaned, not wanting to say good-bye to a friend. "Don't say that. With Tina no longer in the picture, you can relax. Jack Mathias won't hassle you."

"If you ask me, he's too soft for the job."

Charlene Bates strode up to Cassie and thrust her face a few inches from her rival.

"Just what the hell do you think you're doing? I had the okay for the weekend off and now that piss ant Mathias says I can't have it. I've got plans."

"So, do I. Tina okayed my request long before she did yours."

Charlene glowered. "This isn't over. I'm talking to Howard."

"Not even Howard can overrule a decision by Human Resources," I said.

"Fuck them. I *will* get this time off. I have…friends coming into town."

Cassie's eyebrows rose. "Really? I didn't know the Prostitute's Ball was that weekend."

I laughed. Charlie's face turned an interesting shade of red. Her eyes narrowed and she clenched her fists.

To bring the heat down, I said, "You don't seem too broken up about Tina and Janet."

Charlene jerked her gaze from Cassie to me, and then broke eye contact to glance at the schedule. "I neither liked nor disliked Tina. We got along. I barely knew Janet."

Nora, back from the meeting, ambled up with a predatory smile. "Well, Charlene, I see you're flooring the stud section tonight. I'll be watching. You'll be busy, so keep your mind on your games."

"Go to hell. I know how to floor Caribbean Stud and the rest of those carnival games." Charlene tossed her hair back with a quick flip of her hand and strutted down the hall.

Nora laughed. "I think I'm going to have fun

tonight. I can harass Charlene and not have to worry about Tina harassing me."

I stared at her back as she followed Charlene.

"Sounds like you're going to have a super easy night," I told Cassie.

"I wonder if anybody's thought about the soon-to-be new pecking order," she replied.

"What do you mean?"

We turned and slowly walked down the hallway back toward the break room. I glanced out the employee entrance doors. The hard rain had tapered off as the brief storm moved on. I suspected more of the same was on the way.

"Jack Mathias will likely take over Tina's position. One of the current pit managers will be promoted to assistant shift with a dual-rate pit likely to go full. That means a floor supervisor will be bumped up the ladder to dual-rate pit status. And so on."

I stopped and grasped Cassie's arm. "Oh shit, don't tell me Charlene will finally get that dual-rate job she wants so badly."

"I'll bet the little suck-up already has her application on Spivey's desk."

"Why don't you apply?"

She laughed and continued on. "With my collection of pink slips? I don't think so. And while Greg is probably the most competent to take over assistant shift responsibilities, that ain't gonna happen either. He's ruffled way too many feathers."

I saw her point. Since when did competency matter? No doubt Nora would make full pit and either Ralph or Charlene would take her place as a dual-rate. Both of them would make my life miserable. I wondered if they were hiring at the Southern Belle or Golden Hoard.

Twenty minutes later, I pushed open the doors to the casino floor. Noise assaulted my ears. It was a Sunday night and the joint was packed with people getting in those last bets before having to leave for home. Tomorrow was the beginning of their work week.

The Casablanca was unique. All Terence casinos are themed. The movie with Humphrey Bogart and Ingrid Bergman was the inspiration for this place. Even the steakhouse was named Rick's Café Americaine while the buffet laid claim to being the Blue Parrot. Customers found it charming and loved gambling here. Employees weren't so thrilled. We sometimes referred to Howard Spivey as the Prefect of Police.

I wound my way through the throng and entered Pit One. Greg was on the phone at the pit stand. Sandy Hanson, the floor I was relieving, rolled her eyes and hurried to me as I signed on to the first roulette table.

"Thank God you're here."

"Been a rough day?"

"You have no idea. The twenty-five cent table has been three deep since I signed in at noon."

"Nothing like a murder to bring out the thrill seekers. Anything special I need to know?"

"Centerfield on BJ 2 is stoned out of his mind. So far, he's manageable, but I imagine Joe told Greg to keep an eye on him."

Joe was Joe Williams, the day shift pit manager.

"I will. Go home. Looks like you need a drink and a good night's sleep."

"Amen."

As soon as I finished signing in, Sandy beat a fast retreat. Greg handed me two decks of cards to make the change on BJ 2 and shoved six decks into the empty shoe hole on BJ 1. I knew better than to stick the card change with a dealer about to leave, so waited until my team showed up.

Swing shift dealers lined up to sign in and I breathed a sigh of relief when intelligent, competent Doris sidled over to the pitch game on BJ 2. Ben Miller, another dealer who knew what he was doing, tapped out the day shift man on BJ 1.

Thank God. At least blackjack won't pose a problem tonight. Except for the stoner, of course. I trusted Doris to keep me informed on that situation.

With the cards finally changed, I settled into my evening's routine of walking up and down my section, pausing every once in a while to view the action. My gaze frequently shifted to Greg as he also made his rounds. Every once in a while we'd make eye contact and he'd smile. I reacted like Pavlov's dog to the dinner bell, not quite salivating, but coming close.

Girl, you need help. Get your mind out of the gutter and on your games.

I kept my fingers crossed tonight would be relatively quiet. No murders, no upheavals, no nothing.

That hope was dashed ten minutes later when several cries rang out from BJ 2 and Doris called me in a strong voice, "Floor!"

Oh no, now what?

Chapter Seven

Heaving a sigh, I hustled over to BJ 2. The stoner had mixed one too many beers with his joints. He lay face down on the table his overturned beer bottle saturating the felt with what remained of its contents. Luckily, Doris was about to shuffle, so the liquid didn't touch any cards or checks.

I turned to holler for Greg, but he appeared at my side. "I called security. They'll be here in a moment."

As a dealer who handled money, Doris couldn't touch a customer. The same couldn't be said for me. I rapped him on the top of his head with my knuckles.

"Hey, dude! Wake up!" No response. I tapped harder. "Hey, you! If you don't have a room, it's time to get one."

The guy was out like the old proverbial light. I had no idea if the hotel had any vacancies, but he sure as hell wasn't going to nap on BJ 2.

"Floor!" This came from roulette 2, the twenty-five cent game.

"Go on. I'll deal with this," Greg said.

I hustled over to the roulette table where an irate woman and her three companions went into a tirade against the dealer.

"She ain't lettin' us finish betting. She's calling no more bets too soon." The woman glared at my dealer, Donna.

"Donna?" I had confidence in Donna. She dealt a mean roulette wheel.

"I make my pay outs, lift the marker, spin the ball, muck the chips, and make my call before the ball drops," she said.

"Ma'am, you can begin placing your bets when the marker is lifted from the previous winning number."

This was not a new scam. A lot of bettors waited until the ball was ready to drop before chunking chips on the numbers in that section of the wheel. Many new dealers were often lax in calling for no more bets and waving off anything after that call. Fortunately, Donna called before the ball began to drop.

"That ain't fair," one woman whined.

"We should be able to bet until the ball hits the number. Those are the rules," another member of the brain trust asserted.

I wasn't in the mood to listen to a moron who thought she knew it all. "I'm sorry, ma'am, but the dealer is in control of the game. When she says no more bets, there are no more bets."

"Well, I don't know how you got your job. You don't know shit. I wanna talk to your boss," the original complainant huffed.

"My pleasure. Greg!" I backed away and strode toward him where security was escorting the now semi-conscious stoner from the floor. "You want to deal with the bitches on Roulette 2?"

"Bitches, huh? Okay, what's going on?"

I told him what was going down. In the meantime, Donna had continued the game, still calling no more bets just like she had, and with the four women yelling at her with every spin.

"Go watch your other games. I'll put out this fire."

With the stoner gone, Doris had resumed dealing. Ben was whipping cards out of the shoe on BJ 1 at a fast clip, keeping the game moving. My other roulette games, while busy, presented no problems.

A few minutes later, the argumentative foursome left the table, heading for the cashier.

Greg called me over to the pit stand. "They cashed out to the tune of fifteen dollars between the four of them and decided to try their luck at another casino. By the way, they declared Donna was insulting, and you were rude. I was merely obnoxious because I wouldn't give them a comp to the buffet. None of us, of course, knows how the game is supposed to be played."

"Of course. Oh God, please let this night go by fast."

"It won't."

"Anything said at the pit meeting about Tina and Janet?" I asked, eyeing a new player on the pitch game.

"Just the old 'let's pull together in this time of tragedy' thing. You can bet Sheriff Wilcox will have more than a couple of people cruising the casino tonight."

"What for?"

"Listening to what we say, who we say it to, and the reactions."

"Change five hundred!" Doris called out.

I okayed the transaction and clocked the man in. By the time I'd finished, Greg had moved on down the pit. I patrolled my section with my mind only partially on the games. My boss kept intruding on my thoughts. Until I got to one of the roulette games, that is.

"Hear a couple of people croaked in here last

night," a man said to my dealer, Barbara.

"Yes, terrible tragedy." She waved her hand over the game. "No more bets."

"What happened?" The ball dropped.

"Seventeen, black and odd." Barb placed the marker on the number, picked the losing outer bets from the board, and then proceeded to clear the other chips away from the winners.

The man must have sensed I watched. He glanced at me with a frown.

"So, what did happen? Doesn't make a player feel real safe when two people are offed in the casino where you're playing."

Barb shot me a sidelong look as she assembled the payouts.

"We don't know if they were *offed* in any way," I replied. "All of us are very upset."

"Yeah, right. Come on, come clean. I know the cops questioned a whole lot of people last night."

Was this guy a cop here to see how much we'd talk about last night like Greg had suggested? I decided silence was the best policy and didn't answer.

Barb made her payouts, lifted the marker, spun the ball again, and mucked chips from the pile. "Place your bets!"

Distracted by a new spin, the inquisitive guy chunked a bunch of chips onto the board. I helped Barb muck.

"Were you questioned?" Barb asked in a hushed voice, her gaze following the progress of the ball.

"Everyone who went into the office after shift started was. No big deal."

"No more bets," she called out waving her hand

over the board. "Three, red, and odd."

I moved on to another table.

Gayle Simmons, my relief for the night walked into the pit.

"Anything happening?" she asked signing onto the first roulette table.

"Not really. Competent dealers tonight. The pain-in-the-ass players have left, at least for a while."

She eyeballed the table count with the registers in the rest of my section and waved a hand.

"Go enjoy your half hour."

I escaped, only too happy to oblige. The break room had the usual complement of dealers, floors, and pit managers, but the conversational level was severely diminished. Eye contact was at a premium. No one wanted to talk about Tina or Janet.

I followed suit. After pumping change into the vending machines, I chose to sit alone at the end of a long table. The three dealers at the other end ignored me.

So, this is what it's going to be like, huh? I unwrapped my candy bar, took a bite, and popped the top on my soft drink.

Casino rumor mills are often notorious when it comes to accuracy. With so many people in different departments, information is easy to come by. Still, that didn't mean every comment passed on was gospel. For instance, I dismissed the one I'd heard about a housekeeping worker ordered to clean up a bloodstain in the office, thereby insinuating Janet had been stabbed. If there was blood around, the cops wouldn't have let housekeeping anywhere near it.

The poison theory was the most likely, but what

kind and how? I knew little about poisons or how long it takes for a dose to act. I also figured the more obscure the toxin, the harder it was to identify. But then, who around here would have the knowledge and means of obtaining a rare poison? Answer: nobody. At least nobody I knew of.

The how was easier. Since both Tina and Janet had died, the source had to have been the coffee pot in the reception area of the office. If someone had messed with Tina's coffee mug in the pit, the camera would have caught it. There were no cameras in the office— just outside the double doors. So the fatal dose had to be administered there. And it had to be the coffee pot rather than the mug, since Janet was also a victim.

I liked my deductive reasoning. Now all I had to do was deduct who'd done it.

Greg pulled out a chair and sat, a cup of vending machine coffee in his hand.

"So, anybody talk to you?" he asked.

"Not a word. It's kind of unnerving to be a pariah."

He shook his head. "Everybody's giving everybody else the evil eye, especially if they were in the office last night. Sheriff talk to you again?"

"No. Why? Did he to you?"

"At the pit manager meeting before shift. Just said no word has yet come in for cause of death." He leaned forward and pressed my hand. "Dallas, be careful, okay? Don't go anywhere alone if you can help it."

The contact sent a rush of heat through my body. My mind fogged and I swallowed hard to regain control.

"What?"

"Someone killed two people. Tina was the most

likely victim. Janet was an accident."

"But what would I have to fear? No one wants to see me dead."

"Think, Dallas. You may have seen or heard something you don't even know you did."

"You're confusing me, Greg."

He removed his hand and ran it through his hair. "When you were getting reamed out by Tina was there anyone else in the outer office?"

"I don't know. I didn't pay much attention. Shift had just started, Cliff had screwed up, which meant I had screwed up. I was going to buy pink. My irritation level was high."

"They might have been waiting, just standing there, maybe chatting with Janet."

I tried to recall last night. "I walked in, Janet said to go right into Tina's office, Tina told me to close the door, I did, and she made me watch the tape of Cliff overpaying. After that she went into her spiel about what an incompetent jerk I was, how my job hung by a thread, and how it was in my best interests to not criticize management. Yadda, yadda, yadda. I signed the slip, folded it, and left." I paused as a tiny fragment of movement slid into my mind. "You know, I think someone had just entered Howard's office as I walked out."

"Why do you say that?"

"The door was closing."

Greg's gray eyes narrowed. "Did you see who it was?"

I remained silent as I searched my memory, and then answered slowly, "No, but it was a man. I remember seeing someone in a suit—a man's suit—as the door shut."

He leaned back and sipped his coffee. "A man? Are you sure? Women wear suits, too."

"No, this was male—straight sleeve to the wrist, no feminine adornment or anything."

"What was it that Anne said about going into the office to get an apology, but leaving because Tina and Howard were dumping on Ralph?"

"She said both she and Janet were embarrassed, but that was on her first break. I got reamed just after shift started. The timing isn't right. Her rotation wasn't the same as mine."

He frowned. "Just be careful, okay? To please me. Don't use the employees' bathroom or take in the newest sights over in the far corner of the casino."

I liked how concerned he appeared for my safety. It wove into my fantasy life. "Okay, I promise. I haven't used the employees' john since I got promoted."

The employees' restroom and lockers were located down a narrow hallway backstage in the casino. Two public bathrooms were available for customers. One was located near the bar area outside pit 3. The second was in the far corner by the doors reading "Authorized Personnel Only" leading to the employee's domain. It was in an area of the casino only noticed by a few slot players. Most people used the one close to the bar. All uniformed employees were required to use the staff johns, but suited personnel could use the public ones.

Since my promotion, I'd made full use of the public restrooms. The employees' can was often dirty and disgusting. Housekeeping didn't clean in there nearly as often.

Greg rose, then leaned down and brushed his lips

over my forehead. "I'll see you back in the pit."

Stunned and only slightly breathless, I shot a quick glance around the room as he departed. No one appeared to notice. I finished my candy and soft drink. I still had a few minutes left on my break. I decided to stop by the office to see who was taking Janet's place.

I reentered the casino floor and bore right. The office was fifty feet down the room. I pulled up short. The doors were closed with yellow crime scene tape crisscrossing them. A slot attendant finished with a payout nearby.

"Excuse me, but do you know where office personnel are?" I asked her.

"Up on level two in HR. Cops have been here all day from what I heard. No telling when things will get back to normal."

I retraced my steps. So the cops weren't finished in there yet. Maybe there was something on the floor—like a bloodstain—after all. If so, then my theory just got blown out of the water. I shrugged. We'd all know sooner or later.

I ducked into the restroom and washed my hands, listening to the conversations among the few patrons. Most were moaning about their lack of luck, but a few comments were directed at last night's events. I dried my hands and left.

Gayle looked up, checked her watch, and stared at me with raised eyebrows.

"You've still got five minutes left."

"Let Dave have it," I said referring to the next floor supervisor down the pit. "The atmosphere in the break room is downright creepy."

"Yeah, nobody's talking about Tina directly and

people are splitting off into little groups to whisper."

I signed back onto my games and Gayle tapped out the next floor. A few minutes later Greg returned.

The night moved on. As Cassie had predicted, Greg closed down the BJ tables at the far end of the pit a little after eleven. The floor supervisor immediately gave me an extra break.

The atmosphere in the break room hadn't changed. No one spoke or sat near me. Heat surged through my body and a huge weight seemed to press on my chest. If I didn't get out of here, I'd suffocate.

I rose and headed for the exit doors leading outside. The outdoor air wasn't much better—warm and muggy. Off in the distance across the river, lightning flickered. Another storm was making its way toward us. I wanted this night to be over in the worst way.

"Hey, Dallas, what's up?" someone smoking a cigarette under the rain shelter asked.

"Not much. Just getting some fresh air."

I walked into the parking lot taking deep breaths until my nervousness subsided. The murders and the shunning had gotten to me. People I knew and considered friends now pretended I was invisible.

With my break time almost over, I retraced my steps toward the employee entrance. Behind me, footsteps hurried. I cast a glance over my shoulder and saw a shadow slipping between cars. Was I being followed or stalked? Only now did I remember Greg's urgent words of earlier about being careful.

I didn't pretend to be nonchalant, but broke into a trot and hustled across the asphalt and through the doors. Safely inside, I rushed into the ladies' restroom where I composed myself and tried to put the creepy incident out of my mind. *Oh God, please let this night end.*

When I returned to the pit, the action had slowed even more. The long weekend was winding down quicker than usual. I didn't know if it was because they were disappointed no one else dropped dead, or if it was an off night. I asked Greg.

"Could be a combination. It's nearing the end of the month. Money's tight and the suckers aren't staying as long. Who knows?"

Greg lounged against the pit podium. "Shame that extra push fouled up the rotation. I was going to ask if you wanted to…"

A call on the pit phone interrupted our conversation. Greg answered, listened, and then scowled. He hung up and drew a deep breath.

"Trouble?"

"Howard wants to see me on my next break."

"What for?"

"I have no idea."

His relief arrived a few minutes later. Greg hurried out of the pit. My thoughts took a turn for the worse as I remembered Greg's insistence we not mention our pre-shift dinner and conversation.

Good God, is he being re-questioned? And will he use me as an alibi? And if so, what the hell do I say?

Any way I looked at it, I could be next in the hot seat.

When Greg returned, his face was almost expressionless. I sidled up to the pit podium.

"Everything all right?"

He shrugged. "Depends on how you look at it."

"What happened?"

"The sheriff was there. He wanted to know if it was true that I had argued with Tina before shift last night."

"Didn't he cover that last night?"

Greg focused on one of the tables, not looking at me. "I didn't tell him about that conversation. Guess Howard must have informed him."

"What else did Howard say?"

"Tell you later." He strolled on down the pit, observing the floors and dealers.

A few minutes later, Yolanda staggered up to BJ 2 and took a seat setting a beer bottle in the holder. She waved a player's card in the air.

"Didn't take you long to get one of these," I said.

"If I can't work here, I'll play here. Besides, I want to earn enough playing time to get a dinner comp from management. Can't think of a better way to get even." She hailed a passing cocktail waitress. "Hey, babe, get me another beer. This sumbitch is empty."

Her words slurred. She'd obviously been having a good time, not to mention a lot of beer. I clocked her in and wished her luck.

"Don't need luck, baby. I'm gonna be rich soon. I know stuff—important stuff, too, about this stinkin' casino. People will pay attention to me."

I cut a fast retreat. I didn't need a long-winded conversation with a drunk tonight, especially Yolanda Harris. Ten minutes later, she was gone.

"Yolanda give up?" I asked Doris.

"Yep. Bet fifty bucks on two hands, lost, said something profane, flipped me the bird, and took off."

Fifty bucks? Yolanda? I hoped she won the lottery soon. I looked around to see where she'd gone until finally spotting her at one of Cassie's tables in Pit Two.

If she sat there, she was still betting big. I shrugged. It wasn't my money, so what did I care?

Time marched on. More games at the far end of the pit closed. I yawned and glanced at my watch—almost two-thirty. The pit phone rang just as Greg's relief came in. Greg, listened and hung up. With his face set in a deep frown, he strode out of the pit.

"Floor!"

I turned my attention to BJ 1 and solved a minor issue. When I looked back up, Greg had disappeared. The look on his face worried me. It had been a cross between angry and determined.

****

Rain had fallen off and on all evening, but the granddaddy of thunderstorms broke overhead twenty minutes after Greg left the pit. As a rule, the noise level in the casino drowned out any exterior commotion. Not so tonight. Lightning illuminated the outdoors making the parking lot clearly visible through the entrances. Thunder boomed so loudly the chandeliers hanging over the aisles quivered. A quick glance through the glass doors showed rain whipping horizontally along the sidewalk. Trees bent dangerously. A loud rushing noise from outside had everybody looking at each other nervously. Several years ago a tornado had done considerable damage to a casino a few miles away. A brilliant flash, followed by a concussing clap of thunder had me cringing. The lights went out. Startled people screamed.

Power failures are not unusual in Terence County and all casinos have a procedure for dealing with the crisis. Dim emergency lights popped on.

"Lids!" I cried, but already my dealers had sprung

into action. Lids to the trays were slapped over the checks. All dealt cards were gathered and put in the discard box. Shoes sat on top of the trays with the dealers arms folded over them. The roulette games were more complicated due to the configuration of the tables, but my dealers were pros and had the situation in hand immediately.

My job now was to calm the few clearly frightened players left in my section.

"Oh my God, it's a tornado. We're gonna die!" one woman wailed.

"No, no, ma'am," I soothed. "We're perfectly safe. The lights should come back on in a few minutes."

"Hey, the dealer took my cards back and I had a blackjack," a man complained.

"I'm sorry, sir, but all hands are void in a situation like this."

"That's not fair!" he shouted.

That's not fair! God, I hated those words. I knew a dealer who used them constantly whenever she didn't get the schedule she wanted. I certainly didn't want to hear them from a customer.

"Those are the rules, sir, as per the gaming commission," I said trying to keep the irritation from my voice.

"Well, somebody's gonna hear about this!"

"I don't blame you, sir. I'd complain, too."

I conferred with each of my dealers to make sure they had the crisis in hand. They did. Like everyone else, I waited.

Then the lights flickered, came on, blacked out again, and finally came on full as the emergency generators kicked in.

Gamblers all over the casino cheered. The blackout had lasted less than five minutes. Two minutes later the games were once again in full swing. The lightning still flashed and the thunder reverberated, but the rain had let up. The worst of the storm moved east quickly.

It was also the signal for the remaining players to call it a night. Most colored up and headed for the cashier. I breathed a sigh of relief. The night was almost over.

The pit relief glanced at his watch and scowled. I looked at my own. It read a three-oh-five. Greg was five minutes late. Very unusual. During the hubbub, I'd forgotten he'd been on break.

Another minute ticked by. The relief paced, his brows drawn together. Finally, Greg rushed in. His face was pale and his hands shaking.

"Sorry, I'm late, but the power outage caused a few accidents in the back. I was helping people."

The relief gave him the rundown on events and left.

"What happened backstage?" I asked.

He wiped his lips with a trembling hand. "What? Oh, backstage? A couple of staffers walked into doors and two people ran into each other with full trays of food, then slipped in the mess and fell. Time got away from me."

"Are you all right? You don't look so good."

He shot me an irritated glance. "I'm fine. It's been a long two days. I'm tired. Hope Graveyard gets here on time. Watch your games before Surveillance calls down with a problem. No need to spoil a clean night."

"Yeah, sure," I answered a bit put off by his brusque tone. I followed his orders anyway even though questions burned a hole in my tongue.

A few minutes later, a patron raced from the men's room near us and stopped at the entrance to Pit One, yelling, "Help! Help! He's fucking dead!"

Chapter Eight

All heads swung in his direction.

"Who's dead?" Greg demanded.

"How the hell should I know? It's some guy with something sticking out of his back. He's...he's straddling a urinal."

My jaw dropped. What now? Greg got on the phone immediately and called security. A guard rushed up less than a minute later. He and the man disappeared toward the johns. Patrons just rushed for the doors.

"What the hell is going on, Greg?" I asked, ready to cry.

His still trembling hand ran through his hair. "I have no idea, but can bet tonight's gonna be a repeat of last."

Sure enough, within ten minutes, several Terence County cops, including Sheriff Wilcox, rushed in heading for the bathroom. Acting shift manager, Jack Mathias, then called all pit managers with the word swing personnel would assemble after shift in the conference room.

"Not again," I groaned.

"Told you," Greg replied.

"So who's dead?"

He shrugged. "No clue."

"Why is it I see this pathetic job going down the tubes fast? First Tina and Janet, and now some schmuck in the john. Who the hell's going to come to a casino with a death cloud hanging over it?"

Greg paced up and down my section of the pit. "Can't tell. I don't see the cops keeping us for long. Watch your games."

Watch my games? With only four players still hanging around?

"The guy probably won a few bucks, had the checks in his pocket or had already cashed out, went to the can, was followed by some low-life, and killed," I muttered.

"Maybe."

"Surveillance tapes will tell the tale of who followed the guy into the john."

Greg ceased his pacing and stared. For a moment he had a look in his eyes I couldn't identify. Surprise? *Or fear?* I wasn't sure. Uneasiness rippled up my spine.

He took in a ragged breath. "Yes, I suppose they will."

The graveyard shift pit boss walked in to relieve Greg. They moved to the pit stand while I pretended to watch my games.

Greg whispered in my ear as he left. "See you upstairs in a few minutes."

I nodded and turned to Donna on the dead roulette game.

"So, you figure we'll all be looking for work soon?" she asked.

"Whoever said, 'There's no such thing as bad publicity' obviously never worked in a casino. I'll bet tomorrow night we can shoot a cannon off in here and not hit anybody."

"That'll destroy the toke rate."

Boy, would it ever. Tokes—casino parlance for tips to the dealers. The minimum wage salary was peanuts, but the tokes for a week were added up and split between the dealers on all shifts. Some weeks, the toke rate was over twenty bucks an hour. Usually, it hung in there at around ten.

My relief walked into the pit.

"Rumor has it another body has turned up," he said.

"Yeah, some guy got offed in the can. Can you believe it? And the cops are keeping us again tonight."

He looked around the casino. "I have the feeling most of us won't be here for long either. This place is dead—no pun intended."

I agreed no matter how it was meant. Pit One would likely close down to two blackjack and one roulette games by six o'clock. A lot of early outs would be granted tonight.

As soon as he signed on my games, I headed for the ladies room, and then hesitated.

Don't be silly. Nobody's gonna follow a floor supervisor into the restroom and kill her.

I pushed the door open and entered. Cassie stood at the sink washing her hands.

"Do you fucking believe this!" she said. "Another body!"

"I'm ready to believe anything."

She ripped a paper towel from the holder. "I'll save you a seat in the interrogation room."

"Thanks. Greg's up there now."

She left as did I a few minutes later.

Upstairs, the room resembled a carbon copy of last night right down to the buffet table against the wall still laden with unused dishes and silverware. With the murder last night, I guessed the banquet staff had either forgotten or not cared. I pulled out a chair next to Greg. Cassie, Ann, and Nora were also there.

Nora's face was set in furious lines. "What the fuck? Why are we being treated like cattle again? So some guy got whacked in the can. Who cares?"

"Well, I imagine his family does," Ann replied in a calm tone.

"I don't give a flying fuck about them either. This has nothing to do with us. Pull the damned tape and see who followed the clown into the john."

"I'm sure they're doing that now," Cassie added.

She didn't sound as chipper as she had before shift. In fact, there was a tenseness about her that worried me.

"You okay?" I asked in a low tone.

"Yeah, I'm fine, just tired and beginning to think applying for jobs out in Nevada isn't such a bad idea after all. I may not come back."

Nora placed her hand on her protruding belly and groaned. "Goddammit! Where is that half-wit sheriff anyway? Let's get this over with."

Her wish wasn't granted. Like the night before, we were kept waiting, this time with fewer conversations. People sat shifting in their seats or stood awkwardly not making eye contact, uneasiness written on most of the faces. I could almost hear them thinking, am I next?

Forty minutes passed.

Nora groaned again. "For the love of God, what can be taking so long? Come on, already."

She had no sooner spoken when Wilcox strode through the door followed by Dave Billings, the head of security and Jack Mathias, acting shift manager. The one person I expected to see, Howard Spivey, was nowhere in sight.

"Where's our erstwhile fearless leader?" I asked.

"Probably crying in his beer because this casino's going down in flames," Cassie replied.

"You think so?" Anne said, her forehead wrinkling. Obviously, the thought hadn't occurred to her. I sometimes wondered if her eternal optimism and good nature were signs of a slow mental process.

"Hell, yeah," Nora answered, eyeing her with a frown. "Would you gamble at a place where patrons and employees are getting snuffed?"

"May I have your attention?" Billings said from the front of the room.

His expression was worse than grim. The room went silent.

"It is my sad duty to inform you that Howard Spivey was murdered this evening here in the casino."

The entire assemblage gasped. If an emotional shock wave could be physical, then I got body slammed. It reverberated from head to toe. Cassie's eyes widened. Ann clasped a hand to her throat. Even Nora's jaw dropped. Greg's face was blank. He showed no emotion, not even surprise. Then it dawned on me that he hadn't spoken since I'd arrived.

"I'll let Sheriff Wilcox take over now."

The sheriff stepped forward, his expression hard as granite.

"For the record, we are pulling surveillance tapes. We are also reviewing all break schedules for between two-thirty and three o'clock. In a few minutes, I want to meet with all pit managers and floor supervisors in the small conference room across the hall. Everyone else, remain here until further notice." He and what was left of the rapidly diminishing management staff followed.

"But why keep the women here?" Anne asked.

"A woman could have followed him and done the job," Greg said speaking for the first time.

So, the sheriff wanted to see all personnel on break between two-thirty and three? During the thunderstorm? During the blackout? Was that when he'd been killed? I had no idea if the camera's even worked at that time, but then thought they must have if the sheriff could identify the approximate time of death. Perhaps the camera showed Howard going into the john, but never coming out.

When summoned, all supervisory pit personnel trooped into the secondary conference room and stood against the back wall like the condemned about to be shot. Billings passed around several sheets of paper.

"I need you all to tell me who was in the pit between the times mentioned."

I scanned the sheet given to me. It was for my section—Pit One, section one. They started with Greg.

"I was on break at that time. Jim Collins was my relief," he said handing the paper to Jim.

Jim glanced at it and nodded. "The three remaining floors, Dallas, Hollis, and Dave were all present."

"What do you mean by remaining?" Wilcox asked.

"I closed the back portion of the pit around eleven," Greg answered. "Not enough players. Too many dead tables. Some of the dealers took an early out while others gave extra pushes. I closed others later."

"As I said last night, I don't speak casino," the sheriff said. "What's an early out and extra push?"

Jack Mathias answered. "There are two kinds of

early outs. One is natural. Pit, floor, and dealer takeovers by the incoming shift occur at half an hour, twenty-minute, and ten-minute intervals, respectively, prior to shift officially beginning. Those people taking what would be a shortened last break of the night, just clock out and leave a little early.

"Another form of the early out is requested, usually by dealers. These are the people who for one reason or another just don't feel like working. They sign in at the pit stand, and then put their name on a list to go home. If we have extra dealers, they're released."

"Does this happen often?"

"Often enough, especially on slow nights."

"What's this extra push thing?"

"When we have extra personnel, like from closing tables, those who want to work a full shift give extra breaks to floors and dealers."

"I see." He turned his attention to me and pointed to the sheet of paper in my hand. "I take it this was your section tonight, Miss Daniels?"

I cleared my dry throat. "Yes, sir. I remember Donna, Patty, and Johnny were on their roulette games. Bryan was on break. His relief was Janet Linders. Doris and Ben were on the BJ games."

"You're sure of that?" he asked.

"Yes, sir, it was during the blackout and I remember talking to each of them."

Billing took notes as I'd spoken.

"Did you see Mr. Spivey or go to the office at any time this evening?" the sheriff inquired.

"No…oh, wait, yes. I stopped by the office before shift to see who was taking Janet's place, but the place was sealed off. One of the housekeeping staff said the offices had been moved upstairs temporarily. I didn't see Spivey at all."

"Thank you, you may return to the other room."

I nodded and left. As I reentered the big conference chamber, the remaining people looked up. I returned to the table and took my seat. Within minutes, Hollis Brown and Dave Webber, the remaining floors in Pit One, also came back. Greg followed a few minutes later.

"Do they think he was killed during the power outage?" I asked.

He shrugged. "Beats me."

One by one, the pit managers and floor supervisors trickled back in from the small conference room. I gazed at Greg, but he avoided my eyes. His strange behavior and late entrance on that last break rattled through my mind along with the request about not mentioning our dinner date earlier.

And Howard demanded a meeting with him on a previous break—the one where the sheriff had talked to him again. We all have our breaking points. Had this been Greg's? God, I hoped not.

"Think they'll see who did it on tape?" Cassie asked.

"Yeah, let's hope so," Nora replied with a yawn. "The cameras would work, but with that dim emergency lighting, the tape quality would be poor. Anyone on break will be retained for a while, including me, dammit!"

Eventually, the sheriff, Jack, and Billings returned.

"The following personnel need to stick around a while longer," Wilcox intoned.

He read down a list. Anne was not named and

scurried from the room like a frightened rabbit. Cassie was also released. In the end only about fifteen of us stayed behind, me included. Why, I had no idea, since I was in the pit at the time of the crime.

A snarling Charlene Bates sat alone. "Why the hell do I have to stay?"

"Because you're a sneaky bitch and were on break at the time of the murder," Nora answered with a malicious smile.

"Go to hell!"

Sheriff Wilcox raised his eyebrows, but ignored the byplay. "When your name is called, please come to the small conference room. I have a few questions to ask. I'll begin with Jack Mathias."

Jack left with the sheriff and Billings. I turned to Greg. The worried expression hadn't diminished. His lips compressed into a thin line.

"Greg, you never did tell me what happened with Howard—other than the sheriff asking about Tina," I whispered, leaning toward him.

He heaved a sigh, but didn't make eye contact. "Nothing much. Just said he planned on firing me, but decided for the good of the casino to give me another chance."

I breathed a sigh of relief. "Thank God. Do you think the murders are connected?"

"Possibly. I can think of several people with grudges against both of them."

"Shoots down my theory of someone out to rob a patron, doesn't it?"

"Maybe. A thief could have assumed Howard was a guest."

I was silent for a moment until a thought occurred.

"Greg, why would Howard go to the john on the casino floor when there's one just feet away from HR upstairs?"

For the first time, he looked at me directly with a puzzled frown.

"Upstairs? Why would he be upstairs?"

"The cops had the office taped off."

"That was before shift. We had our pit meeting upstairs. All I know is that when I had my chat with Howard and the sheriff, it was in the office. What difference does it make? He's still dead."

"And hopefully soon forgotten," Nora muttered from Greg's other side. She glared across the room at Charlene. "At least that loud-mouthed bitch went home before this crap broke."

"What loud-mouthed bitch?" I asked.

"Yolanda. She staggered onto the quarter table a little after midnight demanding a comp. When I told her she hadn't earned enough points, she got pissy. Called me an ass-kisser and shot me the finger. Said working here had earned her more than enough."

"She's got a point."

"I wasn't in the mood to hear it. If she hadn't been so drunk, I might have given her one just to burn Spivey."

"She was three sheets to the wind in Pit One earlier bragging about how she had the goods on the casino."

Jack reentered the room and walked over to Jim Collins who then left. Ten minutes later he returned.

"Greg, they want to talk to you."

He nodded, rose and walked out the door.

"Well, I'm outta here," Jim said. "See you all tomorrow."

It wasn't until he'd gone that I realized Greg hadn't mentioned the second phone call right before his last break—the one that had sent him out of the pit scowling. Jack approached, sat next to Nora, and wiped his forehead with a tissue.

"You all right?" Nora asked.

"Yeah, but this whole business is damned stressful. Not doing my heart any good, I can tell you that."

"I'm surprised we all haven't had heart attacks," I said.

"Unfortunately, that's a real possibility for me," he said.

"How so?" Nora asked.

"I was diagnosed with the early stages of heart failure a couple of months ago."

"Heart failure! But you look fine," I protested.

"My mother died from it, so I recognized some of the signs like water retention. Sometimes I got shaky and had trouble catching my breath. Doc gave me some meds. They helped, but he upped the dosage a few days ago. Made me kinda dizzy last night, which was why I went home early." He fiddled with the knot in his tie. "If you two will excuse me, I need to talk to Mark Davis. There was some kind of snafu in the craps pit during the blackout."

"Wow, heart failure," I said to Nora when he left. "How old is Jack anyway?"

"Late fifties, I think. God, I hope they get done with us soon. I'm exhausted."

"Must have been frantic in the break room when the lights went out," I said.

She shrugged. "No more than usual."

"I heard a couple of people ran into each other with

dinner trays."

She sent me a puzzled frown. "Not that I recall. I just sat there until the lights popped back on."

Dave Billings appeared in the doorway. "Dallas Daniels, will you please follow me?"

Greg had not come back. I rose and made my way into the hall toward the other room.

Nora's words bothered me. She didn't remember anyone colliding in the break room, yet Greg had given that as the excuse for being late into the pit. I wondered if he had even been in the break room. And if he wasn't, then where the hell was he?

Fear and nerves made my stomach queasy. Was Greg still with the sheriff? Wetting my lips and taking a cleansing breath, I entered the room. Greg was nowhere in sight.

"Please be seated, Miss Daniels," the sheriff said indicating a chair at the small table.

I sat while he fiddled with some papers in front of him. Finally, he looked up.

"Miss Daniels, you said you were in section one of Pit One when the lights went out, is that correct?"

"Yes."

"What did you do?"

I went through the procedure with him.

"And when power was restored?"

"The games resumed."

"What time was this?"

"I'm not sure, but it must have been close to three."

"Do you remember when Mr. Holland returned from his break?"

Uh-oh, those five missing minutes. "Um, not really. A lot of players were coloring up and heading for the cashiers."

"According to his relief, Jim Collins, he was five minutes late and made the comment about helping out in the break room due to a few accidents. He said you were standing right next to him."

Damn, damn, damn! "Oh, yeah, I remember now. A power failure always screws things up."

Wilcox wrote in a small notebook before looking at me again. "I understand you and Mr. Holland are pretty good friends."

"I've known him since he began working here."

"And that was?"

"Three years ago."

"Do you know where Mr. Holland worked prior to the Casablanca?"

"I think he was pitting at the Lucky Deal, just down the road."

"And before that?"

"Not sure exactly. I believe he was at the Big Dog Casino in Atlantic City as a floor supervisor at some point in time."

I had no clue where Wilcox was going with this.

"So, he left New Jersey for a better position?"

"It was a move up the career ladder."

"Thank you, Miss Daniels. You may go home."

I rose and headed straight for the break room without asking why I'd been detained. When push came to shove, I really didn't want to know. I retrieved my purse and jacket from the locker without speaking to anyone. *Time to get the hell out of here.*

I hurried through the parking lot to my car, then spotted Greg standing next to his. His arms were braced on the roof and he stood with his head down as if holding himself up. Worried, I walked over.

"Greg, are you all right?"

He stared at me with concern-filled eyes. "Jesus, Dallas, I'm in big trouble."

Chapter Nine

My heart rate accelerated and I swallowed hard. *Please God, don't tell me Greg killed Howard.*

"What makes you think you're in trouble?"

Greg gazed around the parking lot. A couple of employees walked to their cars a few rows away.

"Not here. Let's go to my place." He pushed away from the car shakily and opened the car door.

"Can you drive?"

He nodded and smiled. "Of course."

I took him at his word and hurried back to my car. Twenty minutes later I pulled into his apartment complex in Swansea. He unlocked the front door, flipped on the lights, and I entered his domain for the first time since knowing him. Our previous meetings had always taken place at my apartment in southeast Memphis. A great breakfast café was just across the street. We'd grab a bite to eat before he left. Occasionally, I wondered if he had a wife or a girlfriend at home, but always stifled the thought.

"Have a seat. I'll make some coffee."

"Don't bother for me. A bottle of water will do."

Greg nodded and disappeared into the kitchen while I chose one end of the sofa. The room wasn't huge, but the neutral colored furniture was tasteful. No personal photos adorned either the walls or the end tables. It was neat, clean, and incredibly Spartan. *Looks like he doesn't plan on staying permanently.*

He returned and handed me the opened bottle, then sat on the opposite end of the sofa. I took a drink, waiting for him to begin. Instead, he just stared at the floor.

Finally, I broke the silence. "Why are you in trouble?"

"Maybe this isn't such a good idea. I have no right to involve you," he muttered.

"I'm already involved, Greg. I'm here, aren't I, so you might as well get it off your chest. Did you kill Howard?"

His head snapped up. "No! I swear I didn't do it, but…"

"But?" I prompted when he paused.

"God, Dallas, I found his body."

"What!" That explained his behavior after returning to the pit. "What did the police say?"

He swallowed and heaved a sigh. "I didn't tell them. I lied."

"But Greg, the surveillance tapes!"

"I know, I know! I was so rattled, I totally forgot about them. I'm hoping Nora's right and the quality will be so bad no one can tell who is entering or leaving the restroom."

"Start at the beginning. What happened after we left Donovan's?"

He ran a hand through his hair. "I got there, poured a cup of coffee in the break room and went to the office, but the crime scene tape was up. A security guard told me Howard was in HR. I was on my way upstairs when I met Jack coming down. He was really upset."

"About what?"

"He's been assistant shift manager for over four years. By all rights, he should inherit Tina's position."

"Let me guess, they screwed him."

"Worse—demoted him back to pit manager. Said they planned on bringing someone in from Atlantic City or Nevada, someone with more big time experience."

"Big time experience? You mean as in dealing with high rollers? Here? In Terence? What half-wit is getting run out of Nevada or Jersey to warrant that? Spivey got a cousin in the business?" Then a thought hit me. "Pit manager? We don't need another pit on swing. Or are they sending him to another shift?"

Greg blinked and drew in a shaky breath. "No, they were going to need one for swing."

"Oh, I guess they wanted to cover for when Nora goes on maternity leave." Then another thought occurred. "Wait a minute, who are 'they'?"

"I think Howard was in touch with the owners. All I know is Jack was madder than hell."

"Never mind, go on. What happened during the pre-shift meeting?"

He closed his eyes, shook his head, and then reopened them. "Nothing much. We were given instructions on not to discuss what happened the night before with anybody—customer or employee. Then he went into this spiel about keeping things running smoothly and everybody getting along. Other than that, it was business as usual. A few hours later, he called and told me to come to the office."

"And he gave you the wonderful news you still had a job, right?"

"The sheriff asked a couple more questions about

the argument I had with Tina and Howard, and then left. When we were alone, Spivey said that given the circumstances, I would have my job provided I stowed the negative rhetoric. One more incident and I was a goner."

"What did you say?"

He gazed into my eyes. "Dallas, I've been in this business since I was twenty-one—that's twenty years! I started out at the Big Dog in Atlantic City as a dealer, and then floor supervisor. Ten years ago I saw the writing on the wall. I'd gone as far as I could go there. Casinos were springing up all over the country. If I wanted more, I had to leave. So I did. I've bounced from casino to casino like a gypsy, never staying anywhere longer than a couple of years. And with each move, the job was not only less satisfying, but the casino reputation-wise a step down. I came to Terence six years ago. I can't go any lower. This is my second casino here. It's also my last. I don't know how to do anything else."

I'd never heard Greg open up like this before. I read the worry in his eyes and heard the fear in his voice. I wanted to hug him and say soothing words about everything being all right.

"So you agreed."

He nodded. "I had no choice."

"I understand, but let's get back to you finding the body. What happened?"

"Howard called later telling me to get my ass into his office on my next break."

"Ah, the second phone call."

Greg nodded. "He was furious. I had no idea what the hell was on his mind. The new secretary wasn't at her desk when I got there, so I went on in. He was livid. It seems someone called the Mississippi Gaming Commission complaining about the casino and how it was being run. The murders also made the commission look incompetent. The upshot was commission members will be here on Wednesday to launch a full scale investigation. Naturally, he assumed I was the culprit who turned us in given that's exactly what I threatened to do last night."

I snorted. "About time they got around to this place, but I can think of a dozen different people who could have snitched."

"I told him the same thing. I didn't do it. He called me a liar and said that as of the end of shift my services would no longer be required."

Oh crap! No wonder Greg was so scared. He had motive out the wazoo.

"What happened then?" My voice had a hoarse tone.

"I left. I needed to be alone and think, so I went out to the car, and just sat there. I returned as the storm broke and stood at the back entrance watching the wind and the rain unable to think of a goddamned thing to do. My career was essentially over. Eventually, I headed for the casino floor, and stopped in the restroom to wash my hands. As I rounded the partition between the washroom and the door, there he was—straddling a urinal, his head against the wall, and a knife sticking out of his back. I was so stunned I just stood glued to the floor. And then the lights went out."

The storm. People assumed he'd been killed during the storm, but according to Greg, he was dead before the power outage.

"What did you do?"

"I got the hell out of the john. Went back through the backstage doors and just stood until the lights came back on. I took a couple of extra minutes to pull myself together. That's why I was late. I never even thought about the tapes until you mentioned them. I was really hoping the body wouldn't be discovered until after shift when we were long gone."

"Exactly what did you tell the sheriff?"

"I knew tape would show me clearly entering the restroom, so I told him I'd gone in, but before I entered fully, the lights went out and I left."

"They might believe you," I said in a worried voice. "I wonder if Howard made any notations about your last meeting."

"I don't know." His voice dropped to a whisper. "You do believe me, don't you?"

Did I? Heat suffused my body causing my stomach to quiver. Of course I did. Greg might get angry, but he'd never kill anyone unless in self-defense. Besides, where would he get a knife? And how would he know Howard was in the can? Or that the lights would go off?

I slid down the sofa and embraced him. "Of course, I do."

His arms closed around me and his lips found mine. This was no friendly little peck. This was a full-blown, world-rocking kiss. My heat level increased, and my heart hammered away. Fantasyland became reality.

Greg broke away to feather kisses across my cheeks. "God, Dallas, you have no idea what hearing you say that means to me." He clasped his hands on either side of my head and looked me in the eye with intense gray eyes. "I want to make love to you. You know that, don't you?"

My breath came in short bursts. "I want you, too. I've missed you so much."

He didn't answer with words, but rose, pulling me up with him, and then once again embraced me. His lips locked tightly onto mine while his hands roamed up and down my back eventually slipping lower to clutch my derriere. He pulled me close—pelvis to pelvis. His erection nestled against my abdomen, hard and heavy. I reveled in the feeling. It was just like old times.

My legs went weak and my knees wobbled. Languid from desire, I hung onto his shoulders to remain upright. Another minute of this and I'd be a puddle of goo at this feet. My nerves hummed and the blood pounded in my ears. I forgot about the murders, the casino, and all else. There was only Greg. I groaned deep in my throat and leaned back, breaking the kiss.

"The bedroom! Where's the bedroom?" I asked with a gasp.

He took my hand and led me down a short hallway and through an open door. I didn't bother to inspect the room once I saw the king-sized bed. I walked to the side of it, turned, and slowly unbuttoned my blouse. The pale blue fake silk hit the floor a moment later. My skirt followed. Then my bra joined the growing pile of clothing. I stood before him wearing a black thong, a pair of thigh-high stockings, and scarlet high heels.

He swallowed hard. "God, Dallas, do you know how sexy you look?"

"Yeah. How sexy can you look, Holland?" I said in a purring tone.

He drew in a ragged breath and quickly shed his clothes. Greg was no Adonis. Not quite six-pack abs or any other sculpted muscles like the heroes in romance novels, but what was there showed great. He'd left his boxers on, the front jutting out. He opened his arms.

I accepted the invitation, closed the gap between us, and reached inside running my fingers lightly up and down the hot shaft. He groaned and muttered something incoherent, then picked me up and laid me on the bed. I had come home.

I raised my arms over my head and struck a provocative pose. "Come on, big boy, give it your best shot."

"Your wish is my command."

He grasped my ankle and raised my leg. His finger traced the stocking from thigh to foot. With a deliberate motion, he removed my shoe and tossed it onto the floor. He repeated the gesture with the other leg. Next he slowly slid the thigh-highs off. They floated to the floor, too. He leaned over and using his teeth, pulled my thong from my hips to my ankles until it was gone.

During this entire operation, his hands had smoothed and caressed my skin, setting off a fire in my belly. I burned like a torch. I reached for him, wiggling my fingers for him to come closer.

"Not yet, baby," he whispered.

He kissed and nibbled his way up my body with his fingers skimming along behind—a light, airy touch that sent my senses reeling and my body quivering. By the time he reached my breasts I had little left in the line of self-control. And when he sucked my nipple into the heat of his mouth, I cried out. A spring coiled inside of me, ready to snap.

Impatient, I pulled his head up to mine and kissed him hard. His hand stroked my thighs until finding that sharp pleasure point at the junction. His thumb massaged.

I bucked and moaned my way through the kiss. Then Greg abruptly pulled back, reached for the nightstand drawer, and withdrew a small foil packet. He handed it to me.

"You do the honors."

Panting with excitement, I sat up and ripped it open while he tossed his boxers aside. Shuddering with anticipation, I lightly stroked his erection then slipped the condom over the tip. I stroked him again before unrolling the thin membrane down a notch. I repeated my actions until he was fully sheathed. During the process, he gritted his teeth and breathed heavily.

"God, you're killing me, Dallas," he muttered.

"Ah, but what a way to go."

He grasped my waist and hoisted me against the headboard in a semi-reclining position, then threw my legs over his shoulders and moved forward until his thighs touched my rear-end. He smiled, caressed me intimately again, and then plunged in.

The sensation was world shattering. Bracing his arms against the headboard, he moved in slow easy strokes. I grasped his shoulders and thrust hard. He gradually increased the pace until the bed rocked and the springs screeched with our movement.

The fire that had steadily grown now burst into a conflagration, the heat searing me both inside and out. I don't think I spoke—at least not anything anybody could understand. I let my body do the talking. I twisted, moaned, and ached for more. His balls slapping my ass was the most erotic thing I'd ever felt.

That coiled spring deep in my belly tightened.

Then with the suddenness of an earthquake, it snapped. Spasm after spasm ripped through me. I screamed and thrust as if touched by a live wire. The contractions kept coming and I prayed they wouldn't stop.

Then just as I was at the peak, Greg let loose with a cry and jammed deep inside me. I felt him pulsating with his release which triggered another couple of seizures. Finally, everything ceased. My legs slipped from his shoulders and he rolled to the side. I panted as I came down from a high I'd never before experienced. This reality was ten times better than fantasy.

"Oh my God," I said when I caught my breath.

Greg lifted my hand to his lips. "You can say that again."

"Oh my God."

"Dear Lord, I missed you, Dallas."

We were silent for several minutes before I said, "I've wanted to make love to you again for months."

"It all goes back to that party where we first met."

"Yeah, I guess it does. The whole thing was a bore until we were introduced. Things picked up from there. Whenever we got together, it was always at my place. I feared you might have a wife or something, but I didn't care. After you came to the Casablanca, I wondered about your personal life. You didn't seem to have one."

"I was married once, a long time ago. She was a dealer in a different casino in AC."

"Any kids?"

"No, thank goodness."

"Where is she now?"

"I lost touch. The last I heard she was flooring on some Indian reservation, but that was seven or eight years ago. It was all for the best. I drank and she gambled. I've cut way back on my drinking. Don't know about her gambling. How about you? Any entanglements since we broke up? You never mentioned anybody special in the break room."

"No. I'm thirty-one and never even been engaged. The boyfriend before you professed undying love until I took an early out one night and caught him in *my* bed with some floozy."

"Can't believe you've never tied the knot. You're attractive and have a great sense of humor. But then, I like brown-eyed redheads with terrific figures."

"We never talked much about the past when we dated. We were more interested in…other things. What happened to your marriage?"

"I drank a lot in those days, Dallas. I knew it was becoming a problem, but didn't have the strength or the motivation to change anything. Then one afternoon I woke up with the world's worst hangover. It was so bad I called in sick that night. I'd never had to do that before. The next day I went to the bank and discovered our checking account was overdrawn. Turns out Sandy's paycheck never made it in. She'd gambled it away. When I confronted her, she denied having a problem. Said she'd win it back in a day or two. We had one hell of a row—just one of many over the three years we were married. That's when she told me she'd been cheating with a floor supervisor from her casino for the past year.

"I packed my clothes and said goodbye. I stayed off the sauce, got a divorce, and left Atlantic City."

"But you still have a drink now and then," I said remembering the party where we'd first met and the wine he'd had with dinner earlier.

He nodded. "I can control it."

I fingered the sheet covering us. His statement concerned me. Wasn't that what all people with drinking problems said?

As if reading my mind, he added, "I hadn't crossed that line yet, thank God. I stick with wine or beer. The hard stuff is a thing of the past."

"I once had an uncle who got bombed every night on beer."

"That can happen. Alcohol is alcohol. But like I said, I got it under control before it became a serious problem. I drink in social situations only, and those are few and far between."

"Like the night we met?" I continued to stare at my fingers busily pleating the sheet, not wanting to meet his eyes.

"Yes. Look at me, Dallas."

I turned my head and stared into his eyes.

"It took me a long time to realize why I drank. The stress of my job and my marriage made me one very unhappy man. Liquor seemed to help, but it was all an illusion. I simply ignored the root problem."

"But you're a pit manager now. I'd think the stress would be greater."

"I'm not in Atlantic City anymore. I'm in Terence, Mississippi. Not nearly the same responsibility level." He paused and drew in a deep breath, then let it out in a rush. "I deal with stress now by being sarcastic and expressing my opinion to anyone who'll listen, which has gotten me into the mess I'm in."

I wasn't ready to discuss the mess. I wanted answers to something more personal.

"Yet, at that party, you kissed me. Why?"

He smiled, took my hand, and brushed his lips over it.

"I'd had less than one glass of wine and was about to leave when I looked up and there you were. As I said, I have a thing for redheads."

"Was your ex a redhead?" I asked as a dart of jealousy popped me in the chest.

Greg laughed. "No, which should have told me something right off the bat. As for you, Dallas, we danced, we flirted, and I kissed you because I wanted to. I was drawn to you and didn't want to let you out of my sight."

"And we ended up in bed."

"That we did, and I never regretted it. Those were the best three months of my life."

Indignation replaced the jealousy. "Then why the hell did you break it off? I was devasated."

"It wasn't an easy thing to do for me either." He dropped my hand and stared at the ceiling, sighing. "After my divorce, I swore I'd never again become involved with someone in the business. The hours suck, and it's hard to maintain a relationship in a casino environment. I worked swing shift. Sandy worked days in a different casino. We rarely saw each other, and neither of us wanted to change." He stopped and ran a hand through his hair. "I'm not surprised the marriage failed. I was just existing until you came into my life. Suddenly, I found myself caring way too much about a woman who worked in a casino. I didn't want to take the chance of failure again. I know I hurt you, and I'm sorry, but at the time I thought it was for the best."

"At the time?" I asked. His words gave me hope. I could now believe it wasn't something I'd done or said to make him dump me.

"Took me a while to realize I wasn't happy. I meant it when I said those were the best three months of my life. I missed seeing you, talking to you, loving you. The Lucky Deal was almost as mismanaged at the Casablanca. I'd been written up several times for my attitude there, too. I finally quit and came to the Casablanca. At least I'd get to see and talk to you."

A bubble of happiness clogged my chest. He cared. He always had.

"But wasn't that like tossing crumbs to a starving man?"

He shrugged. "In a way, but I was willing to eat crumbs just to be with you. I wanted you as a friend. Splitting up people who can be supervised by someone they're dating or married to is a good idea. I thought I could handle a platonic relationship."

"I think you were kidding yourself. You knew that sooner or later the lid would blow off, no matter how careful you were. What was the plan then?"

He hesitated. "I don't know. And maybe you're right—things might have become complicated again."

"They just did," I said in a dry tone.

He ignored my comment. "Tina and Howard's deaths have changed the game. I can't think about plan 'B' when plan 'A' is so screwed up. Sheriff Wilcox is going to arrest me, Dallas. I know it."

"Yeah, I'm afraid of that, too." I rolled over and laid my head on his shoulder. "But I'm here for you, Greg. Your rejection damn near killed me. I walked around in a fog for months. And then one night, I signed in, looked up, and saw you at the pit podium. I didn't know whether to be glad or not. I'd just come to the conclusion I *could* live without you. All I knew was that I'd get to see you on a nightly basis. Guess we both had that to live on."

He stroked my hair and smiled. "Yeah, I guess we did.

His lips claimed mine in a searing kiss. Instinct took over. I knew this would not be gentle love making, but wild and savage. I wanted it that way. I wanted to make up for the three years of seeing, but not touching him. I wanted to claw, bite, scratch, and devour Greg Holland with every ounce of pent-up passion I had.

That's just what we did, thrashing and pouncing until the inevitable conclusion sapped the last of our strength. Exhausted, we lay panting. Words weren't necessary.

I yawned and snuggled down, pulling the sheet up over my nakedness. Greg rolled over and clasped his arm around my waist, drawing me to his side. I heaved a deep sigh. Murder and mayhem didn't count. Greg was back. That's all I cared about.

Chapter Ten

I awoke at noon. Greg was gone, but the smell of bacon and coffee permeated the room. I sat up and stretched suddenly ravenous. I gathered my clothes from the floor and dressed, then found my way down the hall to the kitchen. Greg stood at the stove wearing jeans and a T-shirt. He grinned when I entered.

"Thought this would wake you."

I poured a cup of coffee. "What's for breakfast?"

"You decide."

"I'll test your culinary skills by requesting pancakes."

"Lady, you are talking to the pancake king."

I laughed and took a seat at the kitchen table while he assembled the ingredients.

As he mixed the batter, I couldn't help but think of work last night, and his confession.

I took a fortifying sip of coffee. "Greg, what are we going to do?"

He turned a sharp gaze on me. "Do? You mean about..." His chin thrust in the direction of the bedroom. "Having buyer's remorse?"

"No, no. I mean the eight hundred pound gorilla in the room. Howard fired you, and a few minutes later he's dead. Plus, you found him in the men's room, *then* lied to the police about it. What if he wrote down what went on? What if he called Human Resources alerting them to get separation papers ready?"

He poured pancake batter into the pan. "I don't know, Dallas. I doubt he put anything in writing yet. He wasn't like Tina who wrote notes to herself for everything. And I didn't see anybody from Human Resources at the questioning last night."

"No, but at that time of night HR would be closed. He could have shoved your dismissal into an envelope to be delivered this morning. You can bet someone will mention you got canned—if he'd contacted them, that is."

He flipped the pancakes. The aroma made my stomach growl.

"I suppose I'll face the music if and when the problem arises. A lot of people are pissed off with management. Somewhere, somebody has one hell of a motive, besides me, that is."

He shifted the pancakes to a plate and placed it in front of me. I slapped on some butter, covered them with maple syrup, and grabbed a couple of pieces of bacon. Working swing shift also made for interesting eating patterns. Breakfast at the lunch hour was nothing unusual.

"I guess most of us have a motive in one form or another, including me. Let's face it; I've gotten a butt load of pink slips in the past year. I'm not the best floor supervisor to hit the pits."

Greg reached over and cupped my face in his hands making my heart beat a tad faster. His facial expression softened and his eyes turned from steely to blue-gray as his thumbs caressed my cheekbones.

"Don't sell yourself short, honey. Given the circumstances, you do a good job. Management gave you very little preparation for the task. Know what they gave that day shift dual-rate pit, Mary Holmes? A slip of paper with phone numbers on it in case she had a question. You guys had no training whatsoever."

He released me and tackled his stack of pancakes. I did the same, popping a morsel into my mouth. He hadn't lied. These pancakes were fluffy and had just a hint of cinnamon. *Wouldn't mind eating these every day of the week.*

What did I just think? I stopped chewing and flicked a glance in his direction. *Every day of the week? Am I heading into forbidden territory?* While I'd given the future more than an occasional thought, the word marriage hadn't as yet put in an appearance.

I resumed eating not sure if I trusted my renewed feelings or not. We both wanted the physical, but what about the emotional aspects? I worked in the business. Could Greg ignore the promise to himself? He'd seemed dismissive of his ex-wife, but was he? I'd once heard it said men often kept a soft spot in their hearts for an ex—even if the ex had been unfaithful.

And what about me? Was that drinking problem he confessed to really under control? I'd known women who'd put up with drunks for years hoping and praying the guys would miraculously change. But no miracles had ever appeared. I tried to imagine Greg drunk and slurring his words, or maybe passing out on the sofa every other night. And in the back of my mind, he'd always be the guy who dumped me. Could I look past that? Would he do it again? That would kill me—I mean literally kill me.

Guess this is what love is all about—hoping, praying, and believing in each other to do the right thing.

I shoved the doubts to the back of my mind and devoured half of my stack before returning to the business of last night.

"So, what are we going to do?"

"About my problem or about us?"

"'Us' will eventually work itself out. I'm talking about the murders. What are we going to do?"

"We?"

"I'm involved now—on a couple of levels. I can't just ignore the situation. Neither can you. We need to find a killer before the police decide on you."

"How?"

"For starters, what do you know about Howard Spivey? Where did he come from? How did he get this job?"

He ate a bite of food and frowned. "I'm not sure how he got the job, but I know he's originally out of New York City. Rumor has it he's a former cop."

"A cop? How does that translate into casino manager?" I crunched into another slice of bacon—perfect, crispy yet not hard.

"When you get down to it, a casino manager is just that—a manager. He should have a working knowledge of the games, procedures, and management in general."

"Would he have been a candidate for the job in Atlantic City or anywhere in Nevada?"

"No. Those people are pros and would hire from a known quantity. Someone with a long track record in the business and a background of dealing, supervising, and pitting."

"But not here?"

Greg shook his head. "Things down here are

different. Not as much skill is required because the level of play is lower. Somebody betting a hundred bucks a hand in AC is no big deal, but here it's enough to cause inexperienced pit managers and floors a case of high anxiety."

He had a point. I'd only seen orange checks once on a table. Those thousand dollar babies were kept locked away in the vault. Even five hundred dollar purple checks were few and far between.

He finished his pancakes and shoved the plate away. "I wonder where he did come from. He must have had some kind of casino experience somewhere. Not even the Casablanca would hire an unknown."

"Would Human Resources have that information?"

"Of course. The problem is getting it. I suppose we could just ask."

"No way. Too confidential." I paused to think finally hitting on a solution. "Human Resources had two shifts—from eight until five with a full office staff and from five until two with a skeleton crew. They close up shop after that. Any complaints from Graveyard wait until the following morning. I wonder if we could get in and sneak a peek at the files. They certainly wouldn't give us the information any other way."

"Don't forget Surveillance. We'd be on Candid Camera in an instant."

"Yeah, but I wonder if at four in the morning anyone would bother watching. The office is closed. They'd probably concentrate on the casino floor. The only reason to pull that tape is if something happened."

Greg ran a hand over his chin, a thoughtful expression on his face. "That's true. Plus Surveillance changes shifts at six o'clock. At the end of swing, that camera guy would be tired and ready to go home. He might not be as attentive to a camera in a second floor hallway." His shoulders slumped. "Yeah, but how would we get in? Can you pick locks?"

I drained the last of my now cold coffee. "As a matter of fact, I can."

His eyes opened wide. "What?"

"A friend taught me ages ago. I kept forgetting my keys and locking myself out of my apartment. All I need is a nail file and a credit card. You've seen the doors in this place. Not a deadbolt in sight. Just an ordinary door lock, and probably cheap at that."

"Dallas, I don't know…"

"Look, unless you want to spend time in the Terence County Jail, we have to see those records. Maybe somebody other than an employee had it in for good old Howard."

"And good old Tina?"

"That's another story. We have to wait until the sheriff gets the tox reports. Right now, we have to see those personnel files."

He sighed. "We'll do it together. Right after shift. In, out, and hope no one is paying any attention."

I glanced at my watch. "I need to head for home and change clothes"

"Stop by here on your way back. We'll go have dinner at Donovan's again."

I nodded heaved a shaky sigh, wondering what the penalty would be for breaking and entering—in a casino.

****

I knocked on the door and waited for Greg to

answer.

If I'm going to be here on a regular basis, he really needs to give me a key.

The door swung open and I gazed at a petite, excruciatingly thin, brunette. Her brown eyes narrowed as she stared back.

"If you're selling something, come back later. We're busy," she snapped.

What the hell? Did I have the wrong apartment? A quick glance at the numbers under the porch light said no. I jammed my shoulder against the closing door and shoved.

"Hey!" the brunette yelled. "Whaddaya think you're doing? Who the hell are you?"

"I might ask you the same question," I replied with a snarl.

Greg entered the living room from the hallway. "Come on in, Dallas."

The woman reluctantly stepped back and glared as I pushed my way inside, then turned back to Greg. "Who's this and what's she doing here? We need to talk."

"We've already talked and the answer is still no," he snapped.

"What's going on here?" I demanded. Against the wall, I spied a wheeled suitcase. A large purse sat on the sofa.

"Obviously, you know this person. Tell her to take a hike. *We need to talk!*"

Greg heaved an enormous sigh. His expression was a mix of exasperation, irritation, and just plain anger.

"Dallas, I'd like you to meet my ex-wife, the ever so charming Sandy Wallace—or is it something else by now?"

"It's Berranger," she muttered.

"And is there a Mr. Berranger in the picture?" he asked.

"We split about a year ago," she mumbled, pouting.

"Sandy, this is Dallas Daniels."

The ex-wife? Oh crap. Just what I needed. What the hell was she doing here? Jealousy, that green-eyed monster, threatened to choke me. I wondered what Greg had seen in her. Boney, with thin lips and a pinched face, she had little going for her—in my humble opinion, that is.

She fisted her hands on her hips and now glared at Greg. "Exactly who is she?"

I'd had enough. "I'm his fiancée."

Her right eyebrow rose. "Oh yeah? Dallas, huh? I've never met anybody named after a city before, but then Southerners tend to give their kids weird names."

Oh, this bitch was so going to get my fist in her mouth. *Game on, sweetie.*

"We tend to think of our names as unique. No mundane, run of the mill given names, like Sandy, for us."

I strode to the sofa, picked up her purse, dumped it on the floor, and sat, crossing my arms over my chest.

Sandy turned to Greg. "Not your usual taste in women, is she? I thought you liked the demure, quiet kind."

"He married you, didn't he? And I can be very demure and quiet when the situation calls for it. My mama raised us kids right. It's a Southern thing," I interjected. "We were taught manners."

"Yeah, well you must have hid behind the door during that lesson. It's rude to interrupt two people discussing business. Can't imagine what Greggie sees in you."

Greggie?

"We aren't discussing anything," Greg insisted.

"See, honey, it's not rude when it's a one sided discussion," I pointed out in a saccharin sweet voice. "And he sees all my good qualities. I don't smoke or drink to excess, rarely swear, and even though I work in a casino, *I* don't gamble."

That one hit home. She sucked in a huge breath. Anger radiated from her eyes. "Shut the fuck up!"

"Make me!"

She took a step in my direction. I rose ready to deck the bitch.

Greg quickly stepped between us and glared at her. "Sandy, I'm in no mood to fight."

"Well I am!" I growled.

Sandy abandoned me and turned to Greg. She let out a sigh and put an expression of pitiful pleading on her face.

"Oh Greg, please let me stay." She walked over to her suitcase and began to roll it toward the hallway and the bedroom beyond. "It'll only be a couple of days, I swear. Just until I can get a job in one of the casinos here."

"Hold it, sister. That's our bedroom," I said in a malicious tone.

"Don't you have a place of your own?" she demanded.

"Yes. Here. This is my place, so you'd better find a nice cheap motel somewhere. I'm sure you have more than a nodding acquaintance with those. There are several just over the levee from casino row. Oh, and FYI, we work at the Casablanca. I'm a floor there. Would just love to have you dealing on one of my tables."

"Greg," she whined in a plaintive tone.

"I'll drive you." He grabbed his car keys from the desk and headed for the door. "Dallas, make yourself comfortable. This won't take long."

It better not, buster.

I hurried after him. "I'll be waiting. What would you like for dinner, honey? I'll get things started while you're gone."

To further seal my territoriality, I reached up, grabbed his head in both hands and brought his lips to mine. I was relieved when he responded with a deep return kiss.

"Make whatever is quick, babe." He squeezed my ass and winked. "We might do without dinner entirely tonight."

He hustled a protesting Sandy out the door with suitcase and purse in tow and slammed the door behind them.

I kicked the corner of the sofa wincing as pain shot from my toe to my ankle. I whirled and stomped into the kitchen.

Two plates, two glasses, two knives, and two forks were beside the sink. The operative word here was two. Obviously, Greg had fed her. I picked up one of the glasses ready to hurl it against the wall, then took a deep breath and put it down. I'd just have to clean up the mess.

I glanced at the clock on the stove. *Four-thirty.*

Half an hour down to the motels, dump her skinny ass on the sidewalk, and half an hour back.

For want of anything better to do, I washed the dishes. With each swipe of the dishcloth, my mind conjured up what they were doing, saying. *Anticipating?*

I gritted my teeth. *Stop thinking that way. They're divorced, and Greg plainly doesn't want her here.*

Another glance at the clock—four forty-five. I let the water out of the sink and grabbed a dishtowel.

Why is she here? How did she find Greg? Have they stayed in touch over the years in spite of what he told me? What kind of persuasion is the bitch using to get him to change his mind? And is it working? Will he turn around and return with a triumphant ex-wife? And how would he explain it to me?

I thoroughly dried each dish and put it away. Five o'clock. *Okay, he's shoving her out of the car and heading back.*

Donovan's appeared out of the equation now. I opened the refrigerator and stared at the contents. Bread, lunch meat, cheese, mayo, mustard—the usual ingredients for a sandwich. I slammed the door. No way could I eat. I was too freaking mad, but at whom I wasn't sure. Greg? Not his fault his ex showed up. Sandy? Definitely. Jersey attitude didn't cut it in the South. Most casino personnel who came from Atlantic City had soon learned to temper their comments about us bumpkins. Rednecks didn't appreciate being mocked. *She'll be lucky to get a job in housekeeping.*

A large part of my anger, however, was directed toward myself. I was jealous, and jealousy stemmed from fear and insecurity. Greg and I were just getting our relationship back to where we'd once had it. I wanted it to grow. Never mind that Greg might be under suspicion of murdering Tina and Howard. I knew he hadn't. Still, we didn't need this obnoxious influence named Sandy adding to the stress.

I returned to the living room and turned on the TV. Cable news and reality court room shows clogged the airwaves. I settled on *Divorce Court*. Seemed like an apt subject. Two minutes later, I switched to a news channel. It was a toss-up as to which show had the most animosity—the talking heads or the warring couple. I turned the TV off and paced.

What I couldn't turn off was my mind. I relived every kiss, every caress, everything that had occurred between us for the past few days. Would he decide our rekindled romance was superior to that of his ex-wife? Or would he choose a known quantity over me?

That's it, Dallas—a known quantity. He's been there, done that with the bitch before. They got divorced for a reason. If he hasn't felt remorse over the last few years, why would he do so now?

I wandered past the computer and looked at the clock. Five-thirty. He'd be back any second. I stalked to the front window and peeked into the parking lot. Nothing moved. I paced some more, stopping to stare every couple of minutes.

Not getting any satisfaction from my actions, I sat on the sofa and picked up a magazine—*Fashion Today. Must belong to the bitch.* I jumped up and hurried to the kitchen where I tossed it into the trash. Judging from her cut-offs and tank top, I'd have to say she knew nothing about fashion.

As time stretched, so did my nerves and temper. At

five-fifty, I started swearing.

"Where the hell are you, Greg?" I muttered out loud.

How long would it take to check in to a motel and have a quickie?

"Stop thinking like that! She's not that persuasive and Greg's not that stupid."

My stomach tightened and I felt nauseated. Maybe I should get something to eat after all. No doubt about it, Donovan's wasn't happening tonight.

I stomped into the kitchen and slapped some ham and swiss on a couple of pieces of bread. I had taken my first bite when the front door opened. I abandoned the sandwich and rushed into the living room

"Where the hell have you been?" I regretted the words and the tone as soon as they left my mouth.

Greg rolled his eyes. "Knock it off, Dallas."

"It's almost six!"

"Traffic was heavier than usual. Don't pull the jealousy card on me. I can't take it and it's not becoming to you."

I inhaled a deep cleansing breath and let it out slowly. "All right, I'm sorry, but why is she here? Why now?"

He walked into the kitchen and grabbed a soft drink from the fridge. Suddenly hungry, I picked up my sandwich and took a huge bite.

He popped the top and drank. "She got fired from her last job in some dump casino in Illinois. She migrated back to Atlantic City, but couldn't get hired. While she was there, she ran up some markers at another dump. Rather than pay, she took off. She pounded on my door shortly after you left."

"How did she find you? I had the impression you hadn't talked to her in years."

"I hadn't. She ran across a guy we used to work with while she was dealing in Illinois. He filled her in on my whereabouts. Happens all the time."

"Yeah, I know, but what does she want?" I finished my sandwich and opened my own soft drink.

"She wanted to stay here for a while. I said no. Then she wanted to borrow money to pay the debt owed in Atlantic City before some low-life thugs come after her. I said no to that, too. We argued all through lunch."

"She strikes me as the persistent kind."

"She is, but I can be just as stubborn. I don't want anything to do with her."

That bit of news lifted my spirits. My jealousy didn't miraculously disappear, but it did subside.

"Is she really going to get a job down here?"

He shrugged. "So she claims."

"Better not be at the Casablanca," I said.

"Not to worry. She's a day-shifter all the way. She prefers gambling on swing shift."

"Why'd she get fired? Let me guess, attitude?"

"Nope, they caught her stealing."

"Stealing? You mean like out of the rack?"

Greg nodded and finished his drink. "On roulette. She would palm a check, pretend to scratch her neck, and then let the thing slide down her back to her waist where the tucked in shirt stopped it. On break, she'd remove the money and slip it into her purse."

"And Surveillance noted she didn't clear her hands either before or after going to her body, right?"

"That's about it." He tossed the can into the trash and turned to me, pulling me into his arms. "Now is this catechism about over?"

I dismissed the ex-Mrs. Holland from my mind. Not only was she a bitch, but a stupid one to boot. I snaked my arms around his neck. "Yeah, I guess."

He nuzzled my neck. "Still jealous?"

I nibbled on his earlobe. "A little."

His hands slid down my body to grasp my rear end. He lifted and I wrapped my legs around his waist.

"No need, babe. No need at all."

He walked down the hallway to the bedroom.

****

I left the pit on my last break of the night and headed directly for the staircase to do some reconnoitering. It was two-thirty. The Human Resources office should have shut down half an hour ago. I had a nail file in my pocket and my casino ID/swipe card would work as the leverage if the nail file didn't do its job.

My heart pounded in my ears and my legs suddenly had the consistency of jelly. Gripping the handrail, I paused for a moment to take a few deep cleansing breaths before the top step, and then walked into the hallway as if I belonged. The corridor was empty. I hurried on, turned the corner and stopped. My heart rate increased again. A housekeeping cart was outside the door of the conference room. From inside, I heard the unmistakable sound of a vacuum cleaner.

I hadn't counted on this, but it was something I should have considered. Those rooms had to be cleaned sometime. Walking softly, I peered into the room just as the vacuum cleaner shut off. The cleaning lady looked up and emitted a squeak of surprise.

I thought fast. *Maybe there's a way out of this.*

Greg'll kill me, but I have to have an excuse for being here.

"Oh, I'm sorry. I didn't mean to scare you. I'm a new hire in HR and need some help."

"Yes, ma'am?"

"Well, what with all that's gone on around here the last few nights, HR is really backed up on filing and such, so I volunteered for some overtime. The problem is I left my keys in my desk when I went to dinner and now I'm locked out. Could you possibly let me in?" I tried to sound confused and embarrassed.

The woman glanced at the ID clipped to my suit lapel. They all basically looked alike, so unless she looked real close, nothing showed designating me as pit personnel. The badges bore the insignia of the Mississippi Gaming Commission, but that was *de rigueur*. Any employee who hit the casino floor had to go through a background check, especially if they handled money.

"Yeah, I guess so."

"Oh, thank you so much. I feel so stupid, know what I mean? I just shut the door without thinking. It wasn't until I was eating that I realized what I'd done. I guess I'm still trying to get used to the shift time. This working in the middle of the night is weird, isn't it?" I babbled as I followed her down the hallway.

She fumbled for her keys, found the right one, and opened the door.

I pushed in and flipped on the lights hoping she wouldn't notice they'd been off. The lights would have been on if I'd done as I'd told her.

"You gonna be long? I'd really like to get to this office in the next hour," she asked.

"Half an hour, forty-five minutes tops. Thank you so much."

She nodded and left. I closed the door and turned my attention to the file cabinets along the back wall.

"Personnel files—where would they keep personnel files," I muttered.

A quick look in a couple of drawers didn't produce anything. I glanced at my watch—two-forty. I had to hurry.

"Think, Dallas, think!"

Of course, files with sensitive information would be kept in the director's office. I turned toward the door emblazoned with Roberta Hilliard's name and tried the doorknob. Locked. Without hesitation I slipped my ID from the plastic casing and inserted it between the door jamb and the lock. Like all things at the Casablanca, it was just as I'd predicted, a cheap mechanism. It sprang open in less time than it takes to describe.

I entered, flipped on the light, and headed straight for the file cabinets. These, too, were locked, but my nail file did the job.

If nothing else, Roberta was highly organized. I found Howard's folder immediately, but didn't waste time reading it. Instead I hustled back out and into the small room where the copy machine lived. I waited a long couple of minutes for it to warm up, then copied the entire dossier before returning to Roberta's office.

As I put the file away, I quickly grabbed several other folders and copied them, too. I had a lot of questions about a lot of people—some of it just pure nosiness.

I had just finished when I glanced at my watch again.

"Damn!" Three-oh-two. I was late.

I snatched up the phone and dialed down to Pit Two.

"Holland here," Greg's voice echoed in my ear.

"Greg, it's me. Make some excuse to my relief about why I'm late. I'm up in HR and have the files. I'm about to leave."

"Dallas! We agreed…"

"Don't argue, just do it. I'll be there in three minutes."

I hung up not giving him a chance to chastise me further, grabbed a manila folder from the supply closet, slapped the copies in, and shoved it down the waist band of my slacks. No need for the cameras to see me with a folder this size. If anybody looked closely they'd assume I was four months pregnant. I took a moment to write a note covering my tracks in case Surveillance did see me enter, flipped off the lights, closed the door and hurried toward the stairs. Since I couldn't go into the pit looking this way, I ran into the break room and my locker, extracted the file, locked it away, and then headed back to my job.

"Are you all right?" Helen, my relief asked as I signed back on my games. "Greg said you were sick."

"Yeah, I feel better. Musta been something I ate."

"I can understand that if you ate in the employees' cafeteria."

I laughed lightly. "Tell Rosie I owe her an extra seven minutes sometime," I said mentioning the next floor to be relieved.

"What the hell were you thinking?" he growled in my ear as she moved on.

"An opportunity arose where we didn't have to

break in so I took it. I'll explain later."

He nodded with a worried expression on his face and walked away.

Oddly enough, my nerves were more jazzed now than when I was in HR. My heart pounded and my hands shook. Had Surveillance seen me? If so, had they reported it to Jack Mathias? Could I lie well enough if they did? I prayed the phone would remain silent and glanced at my watch every few minutes. Shift ended in less than an hour.

Finally, Greg's relief tapped him out. Ten minutes later, so did mine. I practically ran from the pit to the break room and my locker, removed my suit jacket, placed it over the folder, grabbed my purse, and headed for the parking lot.

Greg met me at my car. "Well, what does it say?"

"I didn't have time to read it and this isn't the best place to do so."

He nodded. "My place."

He moved off toward his car as I slid behind the wheel. I had lots of personnel files, including Greg's. I slipped it from the folder. No need for him to know I was curious to the extreme. I'd read it later.

I hoped the remaining files would give us a clue as to who had murdered Howard, and perhaps Tina.

Were the two connected? I wasn't sure, but hoped the answer was no.

Chapter Eleven

I beat Greg back to his apartment by a good five minutes. My curiosity as to what held him up was satisfied when he finally pulled into a parking space and exited with a bag from a local donut shop along with a couple of large cups of coffee.

He said nothing as he opened the door and we entered. While I made myself comfortable at the kitchen table, he set the bag and cups in front of me.

"Okay, what have you got?"

"Don't know. Haven't read anything yet."

I reached for a donut. He reached for the manila folder.

"That's one hell of a file."

"I copied more than one," I said through a mouthful of cruller.

He flipped through the pages. "Howard, Nora, Cassie, Anne, Ralph, Tina, Janet, Jack Mathias…you didn't miss many. How did you do all of this in half an hour?"

I gulped some coffee and took another bite before explaining about the cleaning lady while he grabbed Howard's file.

"Dallas, she's a witness!"

"So? If anybody asks I'll just say I popped in to leave a note in HR."

"What note?"

"Before I left, I wrote a note and left it on one of the desks saying I needed to talk to them as soon as possible."

"About what?"

"If they ask, I'll make that up, too." He was worried, which in turn made me worry. "Jeez, will you just get on with it? What does Howard's file have to say?"

As he read, I pulled the folder toward me and picked up the next few pages—Anne Sherman's file.

She'd been hired as a pit clerk when the casino opened. Her background included bank teller for over twenty years. The whole dossier was only three pages long and contained nothing of interest—until the last page. It was a copy of her reprimand regarding the fill snafu of a few nights ago along with a handwritten notation no doubt meant for HR's eyes only.

"Listen to this," I said. "And I quote, 'Mrs. Sherman is a marginal employee who has little to say about working conditions. This is her first write-up. Unfortunately, she frequently talks with what I call troublemakers in the break room. She bears watching. Can I dismiss if she gets another write-up?' It's signed with the initials T. R."

"Gee, I wonder who the troublemakers are?" Greg said, his expression all innocence.

"Yeah, who could they be? I also wonder if Anne knew about Tina's note."

"You mean she went to the office to have it out with Tina about that and not for an apology?"

I shrugged and reached for another donut—glazed yeast this time with multi-colored sprinkles.

"Tina could have told her to mind her own business

or something. A bank teller doesn't make much money these days, when you can even find them what with online banking. This was a salary boost for her. The threat of losing her job could have caused her to do something drastic." I took a huge bite of donut and mumbled, "What about Howard?"

"Very interesting. He retired after twenty years with the NYPD. Apparently, retirement didn't agree with him because he turns up two years later at some bottom-feeder casino in AC as housekeeping manager."

"Housekeeping!"

"Yeah, really qualified to run a casino, right? He moved around a lot over the next five years until he wormed his way into a small gambling joint in the Caribbean as food and beverage manager. Three years later, he left and bounced around at several Native American owned places before ending up here."

"As casino manager. That makes no sense."

"I know. He must have strong armed somebody into giving him this job. I'd give a year's pay to know who and what he had on them."

"The Caribbean...someone was telling me once about having dealt in the Caribbean. Can't remember who at the moment."

"Someone mentions an exotic locale and you don't remember?" Greg asked with raised eyebrows.

I didn't like the snarky tone. "Look, it was when I first started dealing, okay? I can't remember every break room conversation I've had over the last six years. For all I know that person isn't even here anymore."

He ran a hand through his hair. "Sorry, Dallas. But I'm worried. You're right. Sooner or later the sheriff will come down on me. We need to find someone else with a motive."

I shoved the remains of my donut into my mouth washing it down with a big gulp of coffee and grabbed the next few pages in the folder—Janet Washington.

Janet was cleaner than clean. She'd worked all her life as a secretary and had been hired as Howard's assistant when the casino opened. Nothing here.

Greg chuckled.

"What's so funny?"

"Ralph the Rat. Before working here he was a dealer at the Cotton Field Casino just down the road. Before that he was a security guard at a local grocery store in Swansea. He also did a stint as a mail room clerk for a large delivery service headquartered in Memphis. In his own words, he was promoted to assistant manager of the mail room facility for his conscientious work."

"Once a snitch, always a snitch. Wonder why he left such a cushy job."

"Says here he wanted to stretch his horizons."

I laughed. "In other words his fellow workers filed complaints against him."

"Or they set him up to look foolish like what happened here. By the way, his file is stuffed full of attaboys. Prior to all of *that*, he did four years in the Army," he said with a grin.

"Surprised he didn't make general."

Greg tossed the papers aside and reached for another bunch. "Ah, Tina."

"You get all the good ones," I complained and searched through the folder until finding Nora Nelson's file. Finally, something I could get my teeth into.

To say Nora had a checkered resume was an understatement. She worked casinos in Las Vegas, Reno, and Laughlin, Nevada, before moving to the east coast and casinos in Connecticut, New York, and Pennsylvania. Her last place of employment had been on Mississippi's one and only Native American casino in the southern part of the state. The last page was a handwritten note stating that Nora had the qualifications to be hired as a dual-rate pit manager, but was hired in as a floor supervisor. It was signed by Howard Spivey. Her starting salary six years ago sounded damned good and she'd had regular raises at six month intervals.

"Greg, if you don't mind me asking, what's your salary?"

"Fifty grand a year—not bad for Mississippi, but way below Atlantic City and Vegas. Why?"

"Nora was hired on as a floor supervisor at almost sixty and been given raises on a regular basis."

"I've had one raise in three years."

I showed him the note. He scowled. "Wonder how she got the job at a wage more than anyone else?"

"The usual way?" I asked thinking of Charlene Bates.

Greg shook his head. "Not her style at all. Nora wouldn't put out like some I know."

I put her file off to the side. Given her attitude, I was surprised not to find any reprimands included. Maybe she did have something on Howard after all.

"What's Tina's file like?"

"She started as a dealer in the poker room at the Boardwalk Casino in Atlantic City, then moved on to BJ and roulette. She was promoted to dual-rate floor after only five years."

"Thought you said it took a lot longer than that to make the grade."

"It does, but here's the kicker, her maiden name is Cantore."

"Cantore?"

"You're not from Jersey, but Alberto Cantore is a capo for one of the major organized crime families in the state. Or rather he was until he got plugged at his favorite Italian restaurant one night about fifteen years ago. After that she moved on to other casinos out of state, mostly on the reservations."

"So, *she* was loosely connected, not her husband?"

"Looks that way. Other than that, her record is disgustingly clean."

"Wonder who hired her here—Howard?"

"Most likely."

I picked up Jack Mathias's file. He, too, had a long resume full of casinos—some good, some bad. Then one notation jumped out at me—the name of a casino in the Caribbean. Now I remembered. He was the one who told me he'd worked there.

"Greg, what was the name of that casino in the Caribbean Howard worked at?"

He riffled through the papers. "Uh, let's see, it says here he was at the Blue Dolphin as beverage manager."

"When?"

He looked again and gave me the dates. "Why?"

"Jack Mathais worked at the Blue Dolphin as a floor supervisor during that same time frame. He left after only six months. Would he have known Howard?"

"The Blue Dolphin doesn't sound like a large casino so I guess it's possible."

"I suppose with the industry growing like it did, it's not unusual to find people who worked together."

Greg slapped some papers onto the table. "Dallas, we're going about this all wrong."

"What do you mean?"

"We're reading files and while it's entertaining to see some of the stuff, it's not getting us anywhere. We need a flow chart."

"A what?"

"A flow chart—a list of people, where they worked, and when. Then we can couple up who knew who when. I'm going to get some paper. Be right back."

He left the room while I read the last file—Cassie's. The first thing I checked was the date of birth. At sixty-one, Cassie indeed was close to retirement. She'd started her career in Reno and stayed for many years as a BJ and roulette dealer. When the industry opened into fresher territory, she'd moved on slowly working her way eastward—South Dakota, Illinois, Indiana, and finally Mississippi and all as floor supervisor.

A copy of her vacation request was in the file. The dates confirmed what Cassie had told me. Tina's name was scrawled across the bottom okaying it. *So, the mix up came from Tina not remembering. That figures. She was so in over her head.*

I also found a note from HR dated about a year ago mentioning a leave of absence granted for a two week period due to health reasons.

I vaguely remembered that. I think her knees had been giving her a lot of problems.

Next up were the write-ups she'd received over her

tenure at the Casablanca—ten in all. I chuckled out loud. I had seven. *Look out, Cassie, I'm breathing down your neck.*

Then I turned to the last page in the file—another notation from Tina. It was dated the night of her death. As I read I felt the blood drain from my head.

Ms. Severin has crossed the line for the last time. Her abusive language and manner toward management is no longer tolerable. Since I am forced by Human Resources to allow her the time off, which I do not recall having approved, I have no choice but to terminate her. Please have the papers ready when she returns. Tina Rosetti.

Oh my God. Cassie was as good as fired. I remembered her second trip to the office the night Tina died. Had Tina told her what she'd done or merely that HR had approved the time off? I had no idea. *And how do I ask?*

Greg returned with a large poster of Italy, flipped it over and taped it to the wall, then looked at me. "Are you all right?"

"I just read in Cassie's file that Tina fired her. It wouldn't be official until she got back from her trip to California. I wonder if Cassie knew?"

"She may have suspected. There's probably a notation about my confrontation with them in my file, too."

"I'd really hate to see her go. She told me the funniest story about an attempted suicide on a riverboat." I related Cassie's story along with those of the boxmen.

"Everybody has a story. I was at a casino in Louisiana and we had a dealer from deep—and I mean deep—in the bayou. Claimed she was a voodoo princess. Before dealing she'd pull this chicken foot on a chain out from under her shirt and shake it over the table. Said it was good mojo."

"Oh my God, I'd leave that table in a hurry."

"She got fired when she refused to deal to a customer. According to Her Highness, he had the evil eye."

"Let's hope she's back in the bayou sticking pins in little dolls."

He shook his head. "Nope, they had to reinstate her. She filed a claim of religious discrimination. I left shortly after that."

The more I heard about this industry, the more I wanted out.

Greg cleared his throat. "I'm kind of surprised you didn't copy my file or yours."

Guilt stabbed me. I stared at the pages in front of me unable to meet his eyes. "Why bother copying my own file? I know what's in it. I didn't kill either of them, and don't think you did either. Besides, I was running out of time."

He looked at me for a long moment before nodding and turning his attention to the poster. I wondered if he knew I was lying.

He picked up a magic marker. "Now, let's start with Howard."

I shook off my discomfort and read off information while he jotted it onto the chart. An hour later, we had what appeared to be nothing more than a jumble of names, places, and dates.

"I don't get it. How does this point the finger at a killer?" I asked.

"Forget who may or may not have known each other. Concentrate on the facts listed. Howard and Jack worked together not only in the Caribbean, but also in upstate New York outside of Niagara Falls. Look who also showed up there—Nora. Howard was once again Food and Beverage Manager. Nora floored, and Jack pitted. And all at the same time give or take a few months." He leaned back in his chair with a frown.

"What's bugging you?"

"I don't see a reason for murder. What I do see is two people getting good deals at the Casablanca. Nora nails down a floor position with a salary way out of line with the norm for even a pit manager. And Jack Mathias is hired on as a pit manager, also at an inflated salary, and gets a quick promotion to assistant shift. I've seen Jack's work. He's lucky to be pitting. He's a nice guy, but often in over his head with pit responsibilities. He's always asking me how to do something."

"Yet he's an assistant shift manager—or was until the other night. A motive for murder you think?"

"Possibly, but I'm not sure he'd have the guts to stick a knife into Howard's back." He rummaged through the files again. "Tina has to figure into this somehow."

A nagging uneasiness crept over me causing my skin to prickle.

I remained silent while Greg read Tina and Howard's files again. "This is odd. Missed it before. Howard didn't hire Tina." He looked up at me. "Tina's hire date is two months prior to his."

"Well, if not the casino manager, then who?"

He frowned. "The casino owner?"

"Who exactly owns the Casablanca? I know this sounds goofy, but I don't even know who signs my paycheck. It's some unreadable scrawl."

"Let's go find out."

He rose and headed into the living room and his computer. Within minutes he had pulled up the casino website.

"It's a corporation called Casino Management Enterprises. They own casinos all over the country and a few in the Caribbean."

"Including the Blue Dolphin?" I asked. At last, a glimmer of light.

"I wouldn't be surprised. None of these places are what you'd call top of the line establishments." He scrolled down the screen further. "Here are the names of the partners."

I stared, not recognizing any of them.

"Whoa," he said sitting back, amazement on his face. "Look at this—Joseph Karnac."

"Who the hell is Joseph Karnac?"

"He's out of Chicago and rumor had it he was vaguely connected through marriage."

"Connected as in mob? As in Tina?"

Greg nodded. "He tried to slip into ownership with a small casino in AC years ago, but the gaming commission blocked it."

"The mob is *not* unheard of in New Jersey."

"Atlantic City was already established as a gambling mecca by then, and the powers weren't about to let a Chicago connection in on the action."

I heaved a sigh. "It doesn't surprise me that the Casablanca would have some kind of mob ties, but it still doesn't tell us who killed Tina and Howard."

"Howard, Nora, and Jack all knew each other in Niagara Falls and showed up here a few years later. Tina was hired by the owners. Karnac's connected. Tina's connected. Cantore was either her father or an uncle or something. But she isn't connected with the others—at least not yet."

"You think this Karnac may have known Tina's relative?"

"It's possible. Maybe his hiring her was payback for a favor granted some time ago," Greg mused.

"Yet neither she nor Karnac apparently have any connection to Howard prior to the Casablanca."

He ran a hand over his chin. "I'll bet my next paycheck that something happened in New York. Something that allowed Howard, Jack, and Nora to put the squeeze on a third party—like Karnac."

"I'm confused."

Greg drummed his fingers on the desk. "I have a friend in Atlantic City who knows more about the business than anyone alive. Used to work in security and did background checks on casino employees. I'll e-mail him and see if he can dig up a connection between the whole bunch."

"But Howard, Jack, and Nora would have no a reason to kill Tina. Well, Nora hated her and had major contempt for Howard, still…"

"I know, but the connection has to be there."

That prickling sensation once again crept over my skin and a shiver slid up my spine.

"Not necessarily."

"What do you mean?"

"Greg, what if we're looking at two killers?"

Chapter Twelve

Greg stared at me with a thoughtful expression.

"You know, you may have the solution. We can't find a connection between Howard and Tina because there isn't one. Unfortunately, I'm still on the hook for both deaths."

"Their murders were spontaneous," I speculated slowly. "A spur of the moment type of thing."

"Maybe not. Assuming Tina was poisoned, the question is who carries poison around with them on the off chance they might get to use it?"

He had a point. "And who would hang around in a men's room just waiting for Howard to put in an appearance?"

Greg ran a hand through his hair. "Wilcox is so going to arrest me for this."

"Unless…"

"Unless what?"

"Greg, Tina always showed up in the craps pit a couple of hours prior to shift change. We all joked about it. Called it her training schedule. I'll bet whoever went into that office between one-fifteen and two o'clock is her killer. Wonder if Howard had a routine, too."

"You mean he went to the can at the same time every night?"

I shrugged. "Why not? I often tend to eat dinner on

my second break of the night."

"That's a stretch. Someone could have ducked into the john and waited hours for Howard to appear." He frowned and shook his head. "No, that doesn't make sense. They'd be missed on the floor."

"Unless it was their day off. Or maybe it was someone who worked with him ages ago and held a grudge. *Or* a recently fired employee." Yolanda leaped to mind. She'd have no qualms about following Howard into the john and whacking him.

"*Or* it could have been someone who didn't know Howard's position here. The killer takes him for a patron, stabs him, rifles his pockets, finds no checks, and beats a fast retreat out of the casino."

I tapped my fingers on the table. "Boy, I'd love to see the surveillance tapes on this."

"On both of the murders."

"Plus, a patron wouldn't think about surveillance. Having just killed someone for nothing, my guess is they'd simply split and never give cameras a thought. I wonder if Dave Billings would let us view the tapes?"

"Dave Billings is a tight ass, but in this case he and his department are looking bad. The problem is I doubt he'd let either one of us take a peek."

"Well, there's no way I'm breaking into the security office," I said in a dry tone.

Greg sighed. "I'm not even sure those tapes are still in the casino. Sheriff Wilcox probably has them locked up in the Terence County Jail property room."

"I'm not breaking in there either." I tugged at my earlobe. "He did show me some stills the other night. Maybe I could spin a tale about wanting to see more on the theory I might be able to add something to the investigation. Wonder if he had people working undercover at the casino last night."

"I'm sure he had people around just to watch and listen to us."

"I didn't see any strange faces in the break room."

"You might know all the dealers and pit personnel on this shift, but would you know slot attendants, food and beverage people, or anyone from housekeeping?"

Before I could answer, his phone rang. While Greg answered, I tried to put things into logical order.

Assume the mob is involved in some way. Except poisoning someone is not a mob MO.

If for whatever reason they wanted to get rid of Tina, they'd have intercepted her on one of the country roads she used to drive home. A quick bullet to the head and an even faster getaway. The killer would be at the Memphis International Airport and probably airborne before the body was even discovered.

No, Tina's murder was not mob related.

The mob connection makes more sense for Howard. He must have had something on somebody in order to get this job. After all, Karnac hired him, too.

Howard, Jack, Nora, and Niagara Falls. Greg was right. Something happened in New York that set the stage for Terence, Mississippi. I wondered if I could subtly probe Nora or Jack. Nora was sharp. She'd probably tell me to go to hell, but according to Greg, Jack wasn't all that competent. He might divulge information.

While I mulled over the situation, Greg ended his phone call and returned to the living room.

"That was Jack. He's asked that I come in early to discuss casino operations. The head honchos are coming in from Chicago to oversee management. As of now, Jack is acting shift manager."

"I thought Howard demoted him."

"Howard may not have made it official, you know, put it in writing yet—kinda like my dismissal."

"Wait a minute, the head honchos are coming? As in this Karnac fellow?"

He nodded. "Most likely. The murder of the woman you hired as a shift manager plus the casino manager getting it the following night is strong motivation to see what's going on firsthand. Big, bad, Chicago types probably think Wilcox is a country bumpkin and want to make sure he doesn't bungle the operation."

"Or make sure he does."

Greg just looked at me with a raised eyebrow. "An overseer to put up roadblocks?"

"Why not? Especially in Howard's case. A knife to the back could be the mob's way of handling things."

"Not in a crowded casino. They'd do it off premises."

"And don't forget, the gaming commission is also investigating."

He tossed his phone onto the computer desk. "Aw, hell, I'm tired of dealing with this. My mind is fuzzing out on me. It's almost two o'clock and I didn't get a lot of sleep last night. Someone kept me up with fabulous sex."

"Up being the operative word here, right?"

He grinned and held out his hand. "Up and at attention like a good little soldier."

I put my hand in his and accompanied him into the bedroom.

****

I sensed the air of tension the moment I walked into the break room. The events of the last two nights had cast a pall of suspicion over all of us. Pretending not to notice, I made my way to the vending machine, shoved my money in, and retrieved a soft drink. A quick scan of the room showed Nora sitting by herself at a table.

Now is as good a time as any.

I'd rather tackle Jack, but sauntered over and sat across from her. She looked up and stared with a cautious expression. I read fear in her eyes.

"Hi, how're you feeling tonight?"

She hesitated a moment. "Like shit. How else? I'm sitting here wondering who's next on the hit list. I haven't exactly endeared myself to some of these people."

"I don't think you have anything to worry about." I sipped from the can. "After all, this isn't Atlantic City or even upstate New York."

She shot me a sharp glance through narrowed eyes. "What do you mean upstate New York?"

"You know; that casino in Niagara Falls. That was an Indian reservation, wasn't it?"

She continued to stare, and then relaxed. "Yeah. How did you know I was there?"

I shrugged and took another sip. "Someone said something about you, Jack, and Howard having worked in upstate New York together. Strange how you all ended up in Terence, Mississippi."

Her tension returned as she frowned. "Not so strange at all. Everybody ends up together at some time or another. And I didn't really know Howard. He was in a different department."

"Oh, really," I said feigning surprise. "I just assumed he was the casino manager there, too."

"No, he wasn't." She pushed her chair back and rose. "I'm running relief tonight. Better go see if Jack has any last minute instructions."

As she walked away, I took a gulp of soda. Nora, the one person I thought would keep fear to herself, was scared to death. So scared she admitted to having worked with Jack and Howard, although she had distanced herself from the late Mr. Spivey.

Cassie strolled up and took Nora's seat.

"So, where are you spending the night?"

Startled, I stared until I realized she didn't mean my off hours, but my pit assignment.

"Carnival end of Pit One. At least I'll get the early out. How about you?"

"I'm your relief." She gazed around the break room. "Seen Greg lately?"

"What do you mean by that?" Did she suspect we had begun seeing each other?

Her eyebrows rose. "I mean have you seen him since you arrived? He's usually in the break room before shift meeting. What did you mean?"

"Uh, nothing. And no, I haven't seen him since I got here." Technically, that wasn't a lie.

Cassie smiled, speculation gleaming in her eyes. "How about before you got here? Are you two an item or something?"

"Why would you ask that?" I said in what I hoped was a convincing, I'm-so-innocent tone.

The smile broadened into a grin. "Because I heard he gave you a little kiss on the forehead here in the break room last night."

I didn't want to admit to having slept with Greg or to a previous affair. Hell, I hadn't even admitted to myself yet that the relationship had rekindled and deepened. It was happening all too fast even for a fantasy come true.

"He was just being nice because I was so upset about Tina."

"Bullshit. You weren't any more upset by her death than I was."

"Well, I was upset that I was considered a suspect."

Her grin disappeared. "Yeah, I guess I can understand that. I'm sorry."

"For what?"

"For teasing you."

A change of subject was needed. "When do you leave for California?"

"Friday morning right after shift. My flight takes off at eight-fifteen. I'll stuff my bags into the trunk and go straight to the airport from here."

"But you have Wednesdays and Thursdays off—same as me."

"Yeah, but that bitch Tina made me work 'em. Said it was compensation for the time off. I'll complain to HR when I get back—if I get back."

I remembered the notation in her file, but kept my response light. "Come on, you know you love it here. All the thrills and excitement of those high rollers walking through the doors. Can't find that in Nevada."

Cassie laughed and stood. "Dallas, I'm going to miss you. I'd better get going. I have to check in with Jack to make sure he's got the news I won't be here next weekend. See you later."

I'm going to miss you. Sounded like she'd already made up her mind not to return—or had it made up for her?

I looked around the break room. It was kind of odd Greg wasn't here. I hoped everything was all right.

Before I'd left his place this afternoon, he'd insisted I keep the copied files.

"If they do arrest me, they'll search my apartment, but probably wouldn't bother with anybody else."

I'd reluctantly taken the files, along with the chart we'd made, with me. They now lived in the bottom of a garment bag in my closet. I'd piled several folded sweaters over them, just in case, although if the cops searched, they'd find them immediately. I wasn't that clever at all of this skullduggery.

I cruised into the pit. Bob Nolan, a dual-rate pit, stood at the podium. My worry increased. Greg was scheduled for Pit Two tonight.

"Hi, Bob, what are you doing here? I thought Greg had this assignment?"

Bob shrugged. "Beats me. All I know is Jack Mathias called me in about an hour ago and told me to take over Pit Two duties. Said Greg wasn't feeling well."

That was crap. Greg felt fine a few hours ago—really fine. So fine in fact, I'd had to rush home and change clothes to get here on time. Fabulous sex to tide us over until later had sounded like a great idea in the late afternoon. I swallowed hard and bit my lip as I signed onto my games. Something was wrong—very wrong.

Cassie walked up to change out the cards on the Let It Ride game.

"Where's Greg?" she asked.

"Bob said he wasn't feeling well. Must have gone home."

"Do you believe it?"

"Nope. I think he may have been fired. The last time I spoke with him he expected that."

Cassie fanned out the cards on the table and checked them to make sure it was a full deck. "Possibly, but on whose authority? The two people who could fire him are dead."

I hadn't thought about that. "Jack?"

"On his first night as both shift and acting casino manager? Kind of a drastic step."

"Acting casino manager? I didn't know such a position existed."

"The scuttlebutt is both are temporary. I also heard where the casino owners are due in town soon. Rumor has it they're bringing in fresh blood to fill the spots."

That confirmed what Greg had been told this afternoon.

"So why would Jack fire someone if he's not getting the job on a permanent basis?"

Cassie shrugged and moved on to a Caribbean Stud table. "I have no idea. Because he can? Maybe he doesn't like Greg."

"Dallas," Bob called from the podium.

I walked down the pit to stand beside him. "What's up?"

"Go see Jack on your first break."

"Why?"

He shot me a glance and frowned. "I don't know. I'm not in the information loop. He just called and said he wants you in there."

I returned to my section with a churning stomach. Something was up—and I didn't like it.

I helped Cassie change out the rest of the cards. Business was slow tonight. Only two stud tables, Let It Ride, Three Card Poker, and the Big Spin were open. The Big Spin, a game that reminded me of a vertical roulette wheel, would probably close by midnight.

I yawned and hoped I could stay awake. I was working on only a couple hours of sleep. Another pink slip would just about do me in. I needed to keep my concentration sharp. And why did Jack want to see me? Worry gnawed at my nerves. *Where the hell is Greg?*

Cassie moved on to the middle section of the pit leaving me with my thoughts—none of which were pleasant.

My first thought was that Surveillance had seen me entering the Human Resources office. I worked on my story of going there to leave a note. It sounded plausible in my mind.

Gosh, Jack, I went there to talk to someone about all that's gone on the last couple of days. I'm kinda scared. Guess everybody is. I forgot about the time and when I saw the office closed, asked one of the housekeeping staff in another room if she'd let me in to leave a note.

Yeah, that sounded genuine. I breathed easier. A few minutes later the plausibility of that explanation shattered. I swear my heart skipped several beats and my breath stopped in my throat like a clogged drain.

Fingerprints! Oh my God, I didn't wear gloves and my prints are all over Roberta's file drawers!

Oh shit! How could I have been so stupid? I sure as hell wouldn't make it in the spy business. What possible excuse could I give for all those prints, especially since Roberta's office door had been locked? Answer? There was none. I would be as fired as Greg—if he had been fired, that is.

Calm down. Maybe Surveillance hasn't seen anything yet. Maybe Jack just wants to give me a pep talk. He knows Greg and I are good friends and wants to break the news he's been fired to me himself. If he's been fired, I reminded myself again.

I didn't really believe that, so I tried to come up with a story—any story—but my mind was in a deep freeze. Like all casino employees my prints were on file. I had no explanation and was as good as gone.

In spite of my bitching about casino work, the pay was more than I'd ever made in my uneducated life. I'd joined the minimum wage work force as soon as I had my high school diploma in hand. I'd never known anything else. That was typical for Memphis.

When the casinos came to Mississippi, a whole new world had opened for a lot of people. While a dealer's base salary was minimum wage, the toke rate took it higher. For someone like me twelve or fifteen dollars an hour was a freaking fortune. The starting salary as a full time floor was a cool thirty-five grand a year. Going back to the fast food industry with a mantra of "You want fries with that?" was not appealing. Same with stocking shelves or checking people out at the local discount store. Yet, I was totally unqualified for anything else.

Cassie was relieving section one. I had less than an hour to perfect a story. With my nerves on edge I paced my section like a caged tiger. Some schmuck on Caribbean Stud hit a flush. I oversaw the pay out as

Bob came down to okay the transaction. He didn't look me in the eye, which said he'd probably lied when saying he didn't know why I was being called on the carpet.

A minute later, another player got lucky with three of a kind on Three Card Poker. At least, I was kept busy.

Cassie, now in section two of the pit, wandered down toward me.

"Are you all right? You're pacing and not even pretending to watch the games."

I told her of my summons.

"Don't worry. I doubt it's a reprimand. I talked to him just before shift started, too. He said to be on my toes for the next couple of days. Things are disorganized at the moment and he needs our cooperation. It's a cheerleader thing."

I hoped she was right, but it still didn't explain Greg's absence.

Fifteen minutes later, Cassie was signing on my games. She smiled, gave me the thumbs up sign, and wished me good luck.

Nodding, I left the pit with my legs shaking and my stomach churning. I inhaled several deep breaths as I made my way to the office.

Inside, I noticed Jack at Howard's desk. Another man sat just out of sight. All I saw was a couple of legs in khaki pants.

The new secretary smiled. "What can I do for you?"

"I'm Dallas Daniels. Jack asked me to come in on my first break."

The smile disappeared—not a good sign.

"Oh, yes, go on in. He's waiting for you."

Taking one last deep breath to control my shaking hands, I walked through the door, and then stopped dead. The other man inside was Sheriff Remington Wilcox.

"Dallas, please close the door and have a seat," Jack said barely looking up from an open file folder in front of him.

I did as asked and tried to control my trembling.

"As you know, things are in turmoil right now. I need the cooperation of all of you for this casino to remain open. Brass is coming in soon. Changes will be made."

I breathed easier. Cassie was right. This was a cheerleading session.

"I understand, and you have my full cooperation, Jack."

"Unfortunately, there's been a new development."

"A new development?" I echoed.

"I'm afraid so, Miss Daniels," the sheriff added. His dark eyes bored a hole into my soul. "How well do you know Yolanda Harris?"

The question caught me completely off guard. "Yolanda? I've talked to her a few times, but I wasn't what you'd call a friend. More of an acquaintance."

"I see. It's my sad duty to tell you that Miss Harris was murdered in her trailer in Swansea last night. This evening we arrested Greg Holland for the murders of Tina Rosetti, Howard Spivey, and Yolanda Harris."

Chapter Thirteen

My heart squeezed in my chest and I couldn't breathe. Yolanda dead? Greg arrested? Oh, this had to be a nightmare.

"That's…that's not possible," I said with a gasp.

Wilcox's eyebrows rose. "What's not possible? Miss Harris's death or Mr. Holland's arrest?"

"Both! Look, I know Greg. He might get angry around this place—we all do from time to time—but there's no way he'd kill anybody. You've made a terrible mistake, Sheriff."

"He had two altercations with Ms. Rosetti just prior to her death. Mr. Spivey told us. The next night, Mr. Holland had an argument with Mr. Spivey, and then *he* ends up dead. Now Yolanda Harris."

"How do you know Greg had an argument with Howard?"

"The secretary heard raised voices through the door."

I had a hard time processing this. The long arm of circumstantial evidence was slowly embracing Greg. Tears welled in my eyes. I sniffed and pulled a tissue from the box on Jack's desk.

"Why would Greg kill Yolanda?" I wiped my eyes. "To my knowledge, he didn't have an argument with her. It makes no sense."

"She was in the casino last night and played in all

four pits."

I waved my hand in irritation. "I don't recall Greg even talking to her."

"Several personnel heard her talking about how rich she'd soon be—that she knew important things other people would rather not have revealed."

"Yolanda was full of shit! I heard her say the same thing while in Pit One. She'd just been canned the other day, so naturally she'd want to say something bad about the Casablanca. She was drunk, and when she drank, she often spouted off. Belligerence and attitude got her tossed out of several casinos on more than one occasion."

"Thought you said you didn't know her that well."

"I knew her well enough for that! Like I said, she was always spouting off."

"And what was it she said to you?" the sheriff asked.

"Something about knowing all kinds of important stuff and how she'd soon be rich. It was all bullshit. I assumed she was talking about winning the fucking lottery."

"And the important stuff?"

I shrugged. "Who knows? She may have meant the shenanigans that go on in this casino."

"Shenanigans?"

I shot a glance at Jack who stared back with hard eyes.

"Tina and Howard weren't the most competent people to come around the block. It frustrated a lot of us, especially those who'd been in the business for a long time. *They* know how a casino should be run."

"Someone like Greg Holland?" Sheriff Wilcox

said.

"And others." How could I incorporate the information in the files without admitting I'd read them? "If you want to find a killer, take a look at Tina and Howard's casino backgrounds. From what I've heard they both lacked experience for the positions they held."

Jack cleared his throat before speaking. "It's true that Howard never worked as pit personnel. He was a Food and Beverage Manager. Tina worked in Atlantic City and other places as a pit manager. With the expansion of gambling, qualified people are often hard to find. They more or less learn on the job."

I drew in several deep breaths. And then it hit me.

"Sheriff, when was Yolanda killed?"

"We have surveillance footage of her leaving the casino at three-fifteen this morning. Her sister found the body at one-thirty this afternoon."

Oh my God! Greg was off the hook. I was his alibi.

"Sheriff, I spent the night at Greg's. I was with him from the time we left interrogation here until after two this afternoon."

Silence greeted my revelation.

"And he never left you alone? Not even when you slept?" Jack asked.

I turned my gaze on him, answering in a cool tone. "Who slept?"

He blushed and looked away. "Are you and Greg in a serious relationship? Because if you are, there are rules about pit managers supervising wives or girlfriends. How long has this been going on?"

I'd be damned if I confessed to our affair a few years ago. It was none of their business.

"I have always liked and admired Greg. I considered him not only my boss, but a friend as well. The events of the last few days scared me. He was sympathetic. One thing led to another and we...progressed to the next level. I don't know if it's going any further. I don't think he does either, but any way you look at it, I'm his alibi for Yolanda's murder." I glared at Jack before turning my attention back to the sheriff. "By the way, how was Yolanda killed?"

"She was bludgeoned with a bowling pin."

My jaw dropped. "A what?"

"According to her sister, Ms. Harris kept a bowling pin on an end table as a decorative statement."

I stifled a laugh. A bowling pin as décor? How redneck! How Yolanda! Knowing her, she'd probably stolen it from some bowling alley.

I composed myself and stared at Wilcox again. "So, are you going to let Greg go?"

"I find it interesting he didn't supply your name as an alibi when we arrested him."

"Of course he didn't! He's a gentleman and didn't want to get me involved."

"So, as of now, I only have your word you were with him."

"Are you calling me a liar?" Heat spread up my neck to my face. Nothing pissed me off more than being called a liar, especially when I was. In this case, however, I told the stone cold truth.

"Let's just say I'm going to check out your story. Mr. Holland will remain in custody until we can investigate a few more things."

He spoke gobbledygook—a language reserved for cops, lawyers, and con artists. "Even I know you can only hold him so long without filing charges or something. And you have no proof he killed either Tina or Howard."

"Proof? No, not in the usual sense, but we do have an observation from someone who knows him."

"What are you talking about?" I demanded.

The sheriff stared with a frown. "His ex-wife stopped by the station earlier. She claims to have divorced Mr. Holland on the grounds of physical abuse. Says when he drank, he got angry, and when he got angry, he got nasty."

My jaw dropped. "You can't be serious!"

"She says he called her one night drunk as a lord and babbling about some guy named Howard and how he deserved what he got."

I took a deep breath to quell the anger licking along my nerves. I almost succeeded.

"I've had the—um, pleasure—of meeting the former Mrs. Holland. She's a bitch. A vindictive bitch with a gambling problem. She showed up in Terence to crash with Greg and beg him for money. He said no and tossed her ass out on the street. I'm sure if you check the phone records, you'll find her story about him calling her is fourteen-carat-gold bullshit. Plus, Greg no longer gets drunk. Besides, how would she know about all of this?"

Wilcox shrugged. "This is Terence. Two deaths in a casino in two days is a major topic of conversation. She could have heard it anywhere from the motel maid, to a waitress, to a bartender. I'm working on the phone records, but until I can verify things, he stays in jail."

I clenched my teeth and wondered where Sandy was staying. A little road trip might be in order. I'd kick her skinny ass all the way to the sheriff's office where she could recant her accusation.

"I don't suppose you have an address or place of work for Mrs. Berranger, do you?"

His eyebrows rose. "Berranger?"

"She might be using the name Wallace. I think she's had a couple of other husbands after Greg. Doesn't make her story real reliable, does it? Know where I can find her?"

"Yes, and there's no way in hell I'm telling you. I don't need another body turning up."

I saw his point.

"The former Mrs. Holland isn't the only bit of evidence," he said.

"Yeah? What else?"

"Surveillance shows Greg going into the men's room ten to fifteen seconds before the lights went out. Plenty of time for him to see Howard and stick a knife in his back. After the lights went out, the camera shows someone leaving. His time frame is not reliable," Jack said.

"Whose side are you on here?" I almost shouted.

"The same one I am, Miss Daniels. I want the truth."

Jack glanced at his watch. "Take what's left of your break, Dallas. And I'd appreciate it if you didn't divulge this conversation to others. As far as anyone knows, Greg is out on sick leave for a few days."

I rose and glared at both men. "Yeah, yeah, whatever. Sheriff, when can I see Greg?"

"Visiting hours at the jail for family and friends are between one and four in the afternoon."

"Do you know if he has a lawyer yet?"

"Not my concern," Wilcox answered.

"And remember, Dallas, not a word about this discussion," Jack said.

I left slamming his office door behind me. The startled secretary flinched and stared as I stormed out.

In the ladies room, it took several minutes to calm down. I held cold paper towels to my neck and face while breathing deeply.

Greg arrested? Even though we'd discussed the possibility, the reality made me want to scream. That time line, however, might be a problem. He'd admitted stopping to stare in total astonishment at Howard's body before the power failure.

I returned to the pit.

"So, what did Jack want?" Cassie asked.

I didn't want to discuss the past twenty-five minutes. "You were right. Just a let's all pull together kind of thing. Anything going on I should know about?" I asked as I signed on my games.

She gave me a questioning look. "No, not really. I imagine the Big Spin will close soon. The place is really dead tonight."

"Gotcha. Have a good break."

Cassie nodded and left.

I paraded up and down my section not paying much attention to the games. A grand total of six players gambled. One stud table had no one at it. The inactivity gave me time to think.

The time frame problem was Greg's biggest stumbling block. Maybe he could say he didn't notice Howard was dead—or that it was even Howard.

Yeah, that might work. He walked in, saw a guy straddling the urinal, thought he was a drunk, and then the lights went out. Sounds like it could have happened that way.

Why not? He wasn't expecting to see a dead dude. I'd stop by the police station in Terence in the afternoon and ask to see Greg, then give him my theory.

I wonder if he's lawyered up yet. If so, then maybe I could talk to his attorney and...

I stopped my thoughts when another time frame discrepancy leaped into my mind.

Crap! If security did see tape of me entering HR, how would I explain it took almost half an hour to write a note with exactly two sentences on it?

Maybe Greg and I can have adjoining cells.

I had to do something and fast. My gut instinct swore the answer was in those files. There had to be some bit of information we'd overlooked.

I'd read them again as soon as I got home. Hiding within those pages I'd find a killer—or two.

****

"Wow, you're in a hurry tonight," Cassie said as I waited impatiently for her to sign on my games for the last time. It was three-thirty. I had the natural early out and wanted to make the most of it. Besides, only Let It Ride had any action. The rest of my tables were dead.

"Yeah, I'm tired and want to get home. See ya tomorrow."

I rushed from the pit, gathered stuff from my locker, and drove home as fast as I dared. No sense in giving the state of Mississippi or the city of Memphis any extra revenue with a speeding ticket.

Even though I was staggering with fatigue, sleep was out of the question. I unearthed the purloined files and chart from the garment bag, made a huge pot of coffee, and sat at the kitchen table, prepared to read until I dropped.

I started with Howard paying close attention to his original employment application to the Casablanca.

Most of us had filled out the app online and e-mailed it in. Not Howard. His was done the old-fashioned way with a pen. His resume of previous employment was attached. I reread it slowly paying particular attention to his time in upstate New York, but found no glaring red flags. He'd left that casino moving on to another Food and Beverage job in Peoria, Illinois. That job had lasted less than a year. On the surface, other than having worked in the same casino as Nora and Jack, I could find no reason for someone to off him—or he them.

The same held true for Nora and Jack. No reconnections until later in Terence, Mississippi. Co-incidence? Maybe. Certainly Nora thought so, if I believed what she'd said last night. As for Tina, there was no evidence she'd ever known the other three prior to the Casablanca.

Frustrated, I gazed at the flow chart again. If Greg and I had been accurate with our notes, no one had any obvious connections to anyone else. No reprimands, no firings, no nothing. I clenched my teeth and groaned.

Dig deeper, Dallas. There has to be something.

I picked up Ralph's file. Other than being a total toady ass-wipe, nothing indicated any kind of confrontation with Howard or Tina.

Except for the night of Tina and Janet's murders.

According to both Anne Sherman, the pit clerk, and Yolanda, Ralph had been on the verge of losing his toady status. Both sets of information had come via eavesdropping on partial conversations. His file indicated nothing of the sort.

Then a snippet of something said a few nights ago ran through my head causing me to shuffle through the papers in his file again. Ralph had claimed he'd been called into the office for an "attaboy" commendation. Yet according to Anne, he was getting reamed royally. And there was no indication of an "attaboy" in the file.

Of course, the sheriff could have confiscated all of the papers on Tina's desk, which would explain why the blue copy wasn't in his HR file yet.

I also remembered Ralph's frightened expression while awaiting interrogation the night of Tina's death. Or was it *after* he'd been questioned? I wasn't sure.

Putting aside Ralph, I opened Cassie's again. I'd only given it a quick once over yesterday after reading her resume, application, and Tina's inflammatory note. I flipped through the papers slower this time. Nothing of interest came to light until I noticed a couple of pages I'd overlooked earlier near the end. It was the request for a short leave of absence due to a medical emergency and dated last summer.

Casinos are notorious for not having compassion concerning employee illnesses. Any more than three call-ins in a month and that employee bought a pink slip. A couple of years ago a flu epidemic, which spreads like wildfire in a closed environment, swept the through the Casablanca. Try to get over the flu in less than three days. Ain't possible. Damn near the entire day shift had received reprimands.

I did, however, remember Cassie's absence in more detail this time as I read through. She'd told me it was a family thing; that her son had been in an accident or something. I couldn't remember. It had lasted almost two weeks. *I guess a family emergency can qualify as a medical issue. Or maybe she'd used that as an excuse not to inform her friends of a serious condition like arthritis or something. She often complained about her knees hurting.*

I had only skimmed the top sheet earlier. Now I read what was underneath. The papers were from the company insurance provider and had check marks in several boxes for various tests requested and done, none of which I could decipher. Medical mumbo-jumbo was almost as hard to decode as legalese.

The night of Tina's death had Cassie looking like death warmed over. Maybe her condition had to do with her bad knees. Could be the problem was worse than she let on. Those long rotations in Pit One on weekends added an extra half an hour per rotation on her feet. I hoped she was taking meds to help ease the pain.

I put her file aside and picked up Greg's. Subconsciously, I'd been avoiding this. What if there was something damning in his file? What would I do? Tell the sheriff? No way in hell. Ignore it? Much more probable. I had no idea and wasn't sure I wanted to know the contents.

Gritting my teeth and taking a deep breath, I jerked the papers toward me.

Gregory James Holland had been born in New Jersey and was indeed, forty-one years old. He'd dealt and floored at the Big Dog Casino in Atlantic City.

Okay, so far so good. His file matched what he'd told me. I breathed easier.

Then ten years ago, he'd begun moving around. His employment started out with reasonable lengths of time, but those gradually shortened, some lasting only six months. His last stint at the Lucky Deal here in Terence had been for almost two years. A note dated the day he was hired here was attached.

Tina—Mr. Holland left the Lucky Deal of his own accord. A quick call to a friend over there gave me the information that he was frequently insubordinate. If he wasn't such a good pit manager, I'd have never hired him. He could make trouble and bears watching. Make sure he keeps his nose clean. We don't need someone giving us grief about how things should be run. I've had this discussion with him and he's agreed. Howard.

Wow. I wondered who Howard had conned into giving him this information. The reason for an employee leaving a job was confidential. It didn't matter if you quit, got laid off, or canned, all a previous employer could do was verify employment.

I thought back to when Greg had first come here. He'd been affable and had apparently kept his word, but as things had deteriorated at the Casablanca, so had his attitude. The copies of reprimands in his file showed the worsening relationship between him, Tina, and Howard over the last two years with the emphasis on the past five months.

Greg was pushing the envelope and must have suspected the results wouldn't be pretty.

I glanced at the clock and yawned—almost ten. The caffeine wasn't working. I shoved the papers out of the way and headed for bed. My body craved sleep and if I wanted to visit with Greg in the jail before shift, I needed to rest. In bed, my hand patted the pillow next to me. I already missed having his warm body close to mine.

I wondered if Roberta in Human Resources had noticed her files had been tampered with. Had anyone read my note and asked how and when it got on their desk? Had I turned off the copy machine? Or the lights? I didn't recall.

By going to the jail, I could entangle myself in the spider's web.

Chapter Fourteen

I'd only been at the Terence County Jail once in my life. All prospective casino employees had shown up to be fingerprinted for background checks. I remembered it as small, cramped, dirty, and smelling of stale and not so stale cigarette smoke. As I walked through the door, not much had changed, although it did look as if someone had used a broom on the floor.

A deputy sat at a small desk serving the reception area. I glanced at my watch—two forty-five. I'd be way early for shift, and thought about catching a few winks in my car in the employee's parking lot. I had not had a restful sleep. Too much on my mind, and too worried about all of it.

"Yes, ma'am, what can I do for you?" the deputy asked.

"I'm here to see a prisoner, Greg Holland."

"Your name?"

"Dallas Daniels."

He glanced at a sheet of paper on a clipboard next to the blotter. "I'm sorry, ma'am, but I don't see your name on the visitor's sheet."

"What visitor's sheet?" My voice took on a sharp tone.

"All visitors must call ahead to tell us they're coming."

What the hell was this all about? "I talked to the

sheriff last night and he never said anything about calling ahead. I didn't know reservations were required."

He looked up at me with a no-nonsense gaze. "Those are the rules."

"Well, they suck." Sleep deprivation and anxiety sharpened my voice. I realized such an attitude might not get me past the gatekeeper. I softened the tone. "Look, I'm sorry, but I haven't had much sleep and I really need to see Mr. Holland. Please?"

He didn't look sympathetic. "Sorry, no call, no…"

"Let her in," a voice said from behind me.

I turned to stare at Sheriff Wilcox. "Thank you."

He nodded. "Sign in and go through security. Now that you know, perhaps the next time you'll remember to call."

Wilcox turned and strode through a door emblazoned "Sheriff" in gold leaf, and then closed it with a loud click.

Smart-assed cop. How could I remember to call if I hadn't known about the rule in the first place? I shook my head and took a deep breath. I needed another four hours of sleep. I hoped my pit assignment tonight didn't require much focus.

I signed in and made my way across the room to a table where I left my purse to be inspected by a female officer who then put it into a plastic bag and onto a shelf behind her. I moved on to a metal detector. Nothing beeped as I went through. Another deputy escorted me to a large room. Several tables with chairs on opposite sides ran in a long line down the center of the space. A mesh screen split the middle separating the visitor from the prisoner.

Two of the six tables were occupied—one by a man in dirty overalls, and the other by a woman and her three children. They spoke in low tones to prisoners wearing orange jumpsuits.

All in all, the place was depressing as hell.

A door in the back of the room opened and Greg was led in. He wore handcuffs and shackles, but smiled when he saw me. He looked weary and I swear he'd aged ten years in the last twenty-four hours.

As he sat, the deputy said, "You have twenty minutes. All conversations are being recorded both audibly and visually. No touching and no exchange of materials are allowed. When you're done, press the button on the left and someone will come in to escort the prisoner back to his cell. Once he's out of the room, you may leave. Got that?"

I nodded, and the man left through the door again.

Greg and I stared at each other.

"Orange is not your color," I said in a shaky attempt at humor.

He didn't laugh. "What are you doing here, Dallas?"

"Came to see you, of course. I told the sheriff you were with me last night and couldn't possibly have killed Yolanda. Why didn't you tell him?"

He shrugged. "I didn't want to involve you."

"I'm already involved. I told you that last night when we read the…"

"I don't care," he said staring pointedly at the small microphone attached to the screen.

I'd forgotten the deputy's warning. I'd need to watch what I said.

"Well, I…I do. Where were you arrested?"

"Here at the jail. A couple of deputies stopped me in the parking lot at the casino and requested I accompany them here. I knew immediately what was going to happen."

"Do you have a lawyer?"

"The instant Wilcox read me my rights, I asked for an attorney. I met him last night. Some public defender."

"I don't know any lawyers personally, but can ask around. What was the name of that day shift pit manager charged with DUI? Samuels? Stephens?"

"Dallas, don't worry about it. I'll be all right."

"Have you been arraigned?"

"This morning. I was the first case called. I pled not guilty."

The injustice of it made me want to scream. I bit my lip to refrain.

"Of course you did. You're off the hook for Yolanda. If she hadn't been making noise at the casino last night, no one would have connected her death to the others. Still can't see the connection. I'm sure the list of people she pissed off is long. Her big mouth did her in."

"But Wilcox still thinks I'm good for Tina and Howard."

"No thanks to your fucking ex-wife," I snapped. "She called the sheriff and bad-mouthed you big time. By the way, which motel did you dump her at?"

Having a few words with Sandy Holland/Wallace/Berranger/Whatever was still on my mind.

"We parted company in front of the Sleep Cheap Motel. She didn't even say goodbye. Just flipped me

186

the bird and marched into the place. I'm not surprised she's trying to make trouble. I doubt Wilcox is taking anything she says seriously. It's the tapes that are making me look guilty. I'm not."

"I know you aren't, too. I'll bet the surveillance tapes are inconclusive. There are too many others out there with motive. How they could charge you with murder is beyond me."

"When I got here, they questioned me for a few minutes, then I was arrested and read my rights."

"Morons."

"Not necessarily. They're going on circumstantial evidence at the moment."

"They're still morons. You didn't go near the office after one-thirty."

A thought I didn't verbalize came to me. *What if the sheriff isn't sure who murdered who?*

Greg moved his hands as if to touch me, and then let them fall back to the table. The hopelessness of the gesture made me want to cry.

"Right now I want to hold you, kiss you, and make mad passionate love to you."

Heat blossomed in my cheeks. "Me, too. And we will again—soon. I know it. In the meantime, we have to live on memories of last night."

He smiled and nodded. I'd spoken directly into the microphone and hoped whoever listened on the other end was getting his jollies for the day.

"You'd better go now, Dallas."

"All right, but I'll be back tomorrow afternoon, and every other day until they let you out. That's a promise. Can I get you anything?"

He smiled a sad smile. "No thanks, I'm fine for

now."

I pressed the button. Within a few seconds the deputy came in and escorted Greg back to his cell. In spite of his assurances he was fine, I knew he wasn't. The look in his eyes told me he was scared, worried, and not sure how to get out of the mess he was in. That left me in charge.

Still angry and worried, I rose, took a shaky breath, and headed for the door to the outside world. A loud click told me the lock had deactivated. I opened it and walked back to the security desk to retrieve my purse.

My eyes filled with tears. Greg, a man who was becoming more and more important in my life was in dire trouble. I had to help. Without stopping to think, I strode to the sheriff's office door and knocked.

"Come in."

I entered, closed it behind me, took three strides to reach his desk, and stared him down.

"Yes, Miss Daniels, is there something you want?"

"I want Greg Holland released from this jail."

"Not going to happen."

"May I sit?" I asked indicating one of those resin chairs found on any patio. At his nod, I sat. "Sheriff, let me ask you this. Am I a suspect?"

He leaned back, lifted his chin, and twined a pencil through his fingers like a baton twirler. Ceasing his action, he stared right back at me.

"Not at this moment. Tape shows you entering the casino office only once the night of Mrs. Rosetti's death. That was at approximately eight-thirty. Your presence in the pit at the time of Mr. Spivey's murder is also confirmed."

"And Yolanda?" If he didn't suspect *me* of killing

her, then how could he suspect Greg?

He ignored my question to ask one of his own. "What's on your mind?"

"You know as well as I do, Greg didn't kill Yolanda. I think you also know he didn't kill either Tina or Howard. And you couldn't possibly believe an accusation from an embittered ex-wife. *I* think you're using him to give the real killer a false sense of security. I also don't think you have dick for evidence."

"Miss Daniels, don't assume things you don't know for sure. Facts don't lie. Tape doesn't lie. He was in Mr. Spivey's office just before the storm broke, and he did enter the restroom just prior to the lights going out."

I dumped my purse on the floor and scooted the chair closer to his desk.

"Now, we're getting somewhere. The surveillance tapes. The other night you showed me a couple of stills from them. How about you let me see the tapes themselves?"

"No way."

"I may be able to help. I'm likely to know the people going in and out of the office the night of Tina's death better than most. I work with them. I talk with them. I know their grievances and complaints."

"Mr. Spivey and Mr. Billings both viewed those tapes."

"They're management. They wouldn't know the depths of loathing some of the personnel had toward the people in charge."

His eyebrows shot upwards. "Loathing?"

"Okay, maybe too strong a word. How about disgust?"

"Doesn't matter. The answer is still no."

I heaved a deep sigh. "What have you got to lose? If you're trying to link the murders together, then I'm blowing your theory out of the water. I'm Greg's alibi. And take this into consideration—suppose there's more than one killer—one for Tina and one for Howard? Suppose Yolanda was offed by someone totally outside the casino business? Face it, you're running out of time."

"You could review the tapes, and then reveal the contents to anybody you wanted."

"I wouldn't do that. If those tapes show my mother killing Tina and Howard, then she's yours. I want Greg Holland out of here."

I had no idea if I'd gotten through to him. My request was way out of line, even I knew that, but on the other hand—what *did* he have to lose? He was fresh out of ideas.

Apparently, he came to the same conclusion. He stood abruptly.

"This is totally against regulations but follow me. I'll let you see them, but only in my presence. And you will not discuss the contents with anyone. Is that clear?"

Hot damn, I'd won. Good thing I was in Terence, Mississippi, where protocol and procedure could be stretched.

I also rose. "Crystal clear. Where are we going?"

"To a room with a VCR." He led me down a hallway to a small room with a TV set up along with a couple of chairs and a table. "The tapes are in the property room. Stay here while I get them."

His gruff tone said he still didn't like my idea. Too bad. I was determined to see who else had access to both Tina and Howard and when.

The sheriff returned a few minutes later with several cassettes. He slid the first one into the machine and turned it on.

"This is the tape from the night Ms. Rosetti died. I'll fast forward to the time when all the pit managers gathered for the pre-shift meeting."

The camera angle showed the office doors and a portion of the slot machines along either side of it. One by one, the pit managers entered. The sheriff stopped the tape.

"I'm curious what they talk about."

"From what I've heard, not much. Greg told me it's more of a 'let's-have-a-good-night' type of thing with an occasional still photo of a BOLO player."

"BOLO?"

"Be on the lookout for—you're a cop, you should know the phrase."

He waved his hand as if at a bothersome insect. "I know what it means. Why do you use it? What's a BOLO player?"

"Card counters, cappers, pinchers, swipers, slot busters, anyone who may try to cheat. The information is shared by casinos."

"I never knew card counting was illegal," he said.

"Perhaps illegal isn't the right word. Let's just say discouraged. If you're caught, management asks you to leave and keeps your photo around for a while."

"And what are the rest of those terms?"

"A capper adds to his bet after the cards are dealt and he has a winning hand. A pincher does the opposite. Some players are lax about watching their money. A swiper sits next to them and casually takes a check or two. It's real easy on a busy craps table.

"A slot buster has several tricks, one of which is an electronic device that can look like a ring. They hold their hand near the rollers and it sends out an electronic pulse that disrupts the machine. Supposed to make the drums coordinate or something.

"Another trick is to toss a dollar token or two on the floor next to a player who's got a full bucket of coins. Then the culprit points it out to the player who naturally bends over to retrieve the money. That's when the thief snatches the bucket and walks off. Almost all of the dupes jam that found money into the machine. Sometimes it takes them a couple of pulls to realize the bucket is gone."

The sheriff stared with an interested expression. "And how often do these people get caught?"

"Depends on how observant the surveillance guys are. Is there anything interesting on this tape before say, midnight?"

"Not really. People coming and going. Your friend, Mr. Holland goes in around that time."

That would have been for the confrontation he'd had with Tina and Howard.

"Then let's fast forward to when the action happens. By the way, any news yet on what killed Tina?"

"Preliminary call was heart attacks for both Mrs. Rosetti and Mrs. Washington."

Guilt stabbed me in the chest. In all the furor of the last few nights, I'd forgotten about poor Janet.

The sheriff continued. "I can buy one heart attack, but two? No way. It had to be something they ingested. That's why I asked for blood tox screens and analysis of stomach contents along with the cups found with the victims and the coffee pot in the office. I'm still waiting for word, but my guess is whatever killed them will be found in all the items being analyzed. I do know how to do my job."

I squirmed internally, but said nothing.

He restarted the tape. "Let's get on with this."

He fast forwarded it to a few minutes before one o'clock. A boxman entered and left a few minutes later. Yolanda strolled up to the slot machines near the door and plunked her ample ass onto the seat. These were the nickel slots—and I mean real nickels. Twenty bucks could keep a player amused for hours.

Goofy and Daffy went in next and stayed almost ten minutes.

At one-ten Howard emerged and turned left. Yolanda seated to the left of the doors got up as though to follow, then must have changed her mind. She sat back down and shoved another nickel into the slot. At one-fifteen Howard reentered the office. Behind his back, Yolanda gave him the finger.

The clock read one-thirty when Janet left. Yolanda got up again, entered the office, stayed for two minutes, and then emerged resuming her seat at the slot machine. I remembered her telling us she'd overheard Howard and Tina discussing Ralph before "getting affectionate" as she called it. Shortly afterward, Howard left again.

Cassie appeared at one-forty. I figured this was when Tina told her she was cleared for her vacation as per Human Resources instructions. I wondered if Tina had also told Cassie she needn't bother coming back. If so, then Cassie would have walked out then and there not bothering to finish the shift.

Five minutes passed. Yolanda rose and made her way to the doors where she peered through the window, no doubt to see if Cassie was getting the earful she had a few minutes earlier. Then she hustled back to her seat. A few seconds later Cassie emerged and walked away.

"I wish the tape quality was better. I'd love to see expressions on the faces," I said.

"The cameras used to view the tables are top of the line and very clear. The rest not so good."

At one fifty-five, Janet returned. Tina left at two, the large travel mug in her hand.

"Who found Janet?" I asked.

"Housekeeping. The guy walked in to empty wastebaskets around three o'clock and found her on the floor near her desk. It looked as if she knew something was wrong and tried to get help."

"Wonder why she didn't call someone. The phone was just inches away."

He inhaled a deep breath. "Maybe she didn't know who to call at that hour and thought someone on the floor would assist." Sheriff Wilcox rewound the tape and pulled it from the VCR. "Well, anything to add?"

"No, I'm sorry. Everyone who admitted to being there was. I was hoping a new face would pop up. What doesn't pop up is Greg Holland. If poison was in the coffee pot, then surely someone would have drunk it earlier."

"Don't know that for sure. It's pure conjecture."

"My theory makes more sense." I sighed. "What about tape from last night?"

"I've got two tapes—one from the same angle after we released the office, and one from the area near the men's room," he said shoving another tape into the slot.

"This is the office."

Not a whole lot happened other than Greg going in a little after midnight and again at two-thirty. He emerged ten minutes after his last visit and took off in the direction of the break room. Howard came out almost immediately. The time read two-forty-one.

Sheriff Wilcox stopped this tape. "That's all. Here's the one from near the men's room."

He removed tape one and slid this one in, fast forwarding it to a few seconds after Howard left the office. It showed Greg striding fast and pushing the backstage doors open with a hard shove.

"I'd say that is one angry man. I don't suppose you'd like to tell me why?" the sheriff asked.

"I don't know. Greg didn't say and with Howard dead, I totally forgot to ask." Good thing I wasn't hooked up to a lie detector. My heart had accelerated and a bead of sweat formed along my hairline. I clenched my hands to keep them from trembling.

Howard came into the frame entering the men's room. Two minutes later, another man left. At exactly two fifty-five Greg entered, and then ten seconds later, the lights went out.

Sure enough, the camera dimmed to a fuzzy darkness. A shadow was seen leaving the john and heading for the break room doors. Then the emergency lights kicked in. The picture improved slightly, but didn't come back to full imaging until power was restored.

"That's it," the sheriff said.

"Who was that other guy—the one who came out right after Howard went in?"

"A player, I suppose. No one we talked to seemed

to recognize him."

"Do you have any idea where he was playing or when he entered the john?"

"Wouldn't know about the playing part, but let's backtrack the film and see when he goes in."

The tape fast-tracked back for over an hour before the man appeared. Meanwhile, other patrons came and went.

"That's odd. Who spends over an hour in the can?" Sheriff Wilcox muttered.

"You've obviously never eaten in the employee's cafeteria. Sheriff, look at his clothes. It's late April and the weather the last few days has been unusually warm and muggy. He's wearing one of those Indiana Jones type hats and a long coat—almost to his knees—with the collar turned up. Looks like a disguise to me."

I was certain this guy was Howard's killer. I wanted to cry with relief. Greg just might be off the hook for this, too.

Sheriff Wilcox jerked out his cell phone and dialed while I stared at the image of a tall man on the paused tape. The long coat hid his body size, but he looked well-fed. Something about this guy looked familiar, but I couldn't put my finger on it.

"That's right, Mr. Billings, I want all tapes from the entrances and the parking lots during swing shift on Sunday night. I'll be in to view them shortly…I'll explain when I get there." He hung up and rose. "Miss Daniels, thank you for your help, but I've got work to do."

"What about Greg? Surely this proves he didn't kill Howard."

"It proves no such thing. He could still have

stabbed Mr. Spivey before the lights went out."

"With what? I didn't see a knife in his hand."

"The murder weapon was a steak knife from the casino. Even had the name of the place etched in the handle. Could have had it in his pocket."

"The unattended buffet," I said slowly. "The conference room the night Tina died must have been used earlier in the evening, but the buffet hadn't been completely removed. Everything was the same way when Howard bought it. I remember seeing unused plates, forks, and knives in bins."

"Seems possible."

I gave him the theory we'd all brandished around the table the night Howard had been murdered.

"You mean someone goes into the bathroom and waits for over an hour before attacking someone for a few chips? Sorry to burst your bubble, but this guy could have been waiting for Mr. Spivey specifically."

"I don't buy that. The guy goes into the john with the intention of robbing a patron, but has to work up the courage to do it, so he hides in a stall. Finally, Howard walks in. They're alone. He rushes out and attacks. Maybe Howard fights back, but this guy is strong, shoves him against the wall and stabs him. When he finds out there's no money, he splits."

I mentally patted myself on the back. This sounded like something a half-way decent lawyer would say. What was it called? Yeah, reasonable doubt.

"And the knife from the steakhouse?" he asked.

"For all we know, the guy ate there."

"Maybe, maybe not. That's why I need to see those other tapes. Goodbye, Miss Daniels."

He escorted me to my car and watched until I

drove away. I glanced in my rearview mirror. Wilcox may have looked competent, but not checking out the guy leaving the john a few minutes after Howard entered was sloppy. The guy had tunnel vision—narrow and focused on one person. Greg was still in custody, but I knew in my heart he'd be out by this time tomorrow.

Pride at actually helping lifted my spirits. I'd finally done something no one could fault—except the unknown man on tape, of course.

Chapter Fifteen

My dashboard clock read four fifty-five. I had three hours to kill before shift, so against my better judgment, I pulled into the parking lot of the Southern Belle, the casino next to the Casablanca. The exterior resembled Tara from *Gone with the Wind*. The interior was blessed with large murals of scenes from the movie, deep claret red carpet, and crystal chandeliers. It was bright and cheerful. When I gambled, this was my casino of choice. It was the most elegant in Terence.

Patrons were few. The daytime rush had ended and the evening rush had not yet begun. I sidled up to a dead five-dollar single deck pitch game and took a seat on the end. We in the business called this position third base, since it was the last card dealt before the dealer's.

"Hi, Dallas, long time, no see," the dealer greeted.

He'd worked with me at the Casablanca when it had first opened. Several good dealers had moved on to more reasonably run casinos.

"Hey, Nate, what's up?" I tossed two twenties and a ten onto the table.

"Not much. Sounds like you guys have had a lot of action." He picked up the money, spread it out in front of him for the cameras to see, and counted out ten red checks.

"It's been hell on wheels," I replied as he stuffed my fifty bucks into the lock box and pushed my checks toward me.

"Is it true old Howard got snuffed in the can?"

"Yep." I tossed one of the nickel checks back to him. "Change." He gave me five white dollar checks in return.

"Kind of a fitting place. Poetic justice or something like that. Heard Tina the Terrible had a heart attack and croaked off the night before that."

"When it rains, it pours."

I placed a red check in the betting circle and a white one just in front of it as a tip. If I won, so did Nate. Always take care of the dealer.

"Come on and deal, let's see how good you are tonight."

While he shuffled two more players joined me. I ordered a bottle of water from the cocktail waitress and tipped her a dollar bill. Always tip a cocktail in cash whenever possible. It guarantees good service.

An hour and a half later, I cashed out three hundred bucks and armed with a comp from the pit manager— also a former Casablanca employee—ate at the Belle's excellent buffet.

Later, while sitting in the break room at the Casablanca, I wondered why I hadn't pulled up stakes and gone to the Belle, too. The lure of a promotion to floor had been strong. Visions of pitting had danced in my head. Stupid, of course. I'd never have that kind of experience, not even for Terence.

"You're here early," Cassie said. She plopped her enormous purse on the end of the table and turned toward her locker.

"Yeah, I spent a little time over at the Belle and had dinner."

"Ah, the Southern Belle. I should have applied there instead of this dump. Not being from the South, I didn't recognize the charm," she said over her shoulder.

A couple of day shift dealers walked past pushing and shoving each other in horse play. One bumped into the table hard and his hand hit Cassie's purse sending it flying onto the floor. The closing snap was open and the contents flew everywhere.

"Hey, assholes, watch it!" she yelled.

"Sorry," one mumbled before moving on with his friend leaving the mess behind.

"Double assholes," Cassie hollered again as she stooped to pick up the items.

I helped, snagging her wallet and cell and handing them to her. I then crawled under the table to fetch a compact, what looked like a bottle of eye drops, two tubes of lipstick, a business card holder, an agenda, and a couple of pens.

"Thanks," she muttered when I handed them to her. She dropped the small bottle into her pocket, shoved the rest of the stuff into her purse and jammed it into the locker, slamming it shut, then glared at the break room door. "Boy, I hope their last twenty minutes on the tables is in my section."

"It won't be. They're craps dealers."

"Bastards."

"Any idea where you are tonight?"

"No, and I don't care."

"Wow, someone's in a surly mood this evening."

"You would be, too, if you had to work your days off. Tonight's supposed to be my Friday."

"Oh well, look on the bright side—you're going to California for a weekend."

Cassie smiled. "Yeah, the bright side. Where's Greg?"

I shrugged not knowing what to say. Charlene Bates sauntered up.

"What's this I hear about Holland being arrested?"

"Arrested?" Cassie said her eyebrows rising almost off her forehead.

"Yeah, last night before shift one of the day people saw him talking to a couple of cops in the parking lot. Hasn't been seen since."

Cassie stared at me. I shifted my gaze to the table and drummed my fingers on it.

"I also heard where that loud-mouthed bitch Harris was sent to that great casino cashier cage in the sky."

My friend and mentor caught an audible breath. "You mean as in dead?"

"Yeah."

I wanted to get out of the room in the worst way. I stood abruptly.

"Don't listen to idle gossip. Excuse me. I have to check my assignment for the night."

I walked away on shaky legs. So the word was out, and Charlie-The-Ass-Kisser would make sure it spread. I stood in front of the assignment board and tried to focus through the tears welling in my eyes. Everyone would assume Greg was guilty. That was human nature. If you get arrested, there must be a reason. Footsteps echoed, and then stopped next to me.

"Is it true?" Cassie asked in a low tone.

"About Greg? Yes. Same with Yolanda."

"Oh my God. This is insane. Greg wouldn't have killed Tina or Yolanda. Howard I'm not so sure about."

I whirled to face her. "Greg wouldn't kill

anybody!"

"Face facts, Dallas. We don't know what went on in the woodshed, but being called in several times in two days tells me he was getting spanked pretty damned hard. I bet he had one hell of a motive."

"He's not the only one. So did you!"

She shot me a hard glare. "Me? What are you talking about?"

I swallowed to calm my temper and reminded myself I wasn't supposed to know about the note in the file.

"That…that thing with your time off."

She waved a hand. "Old news. She made me work on my days off, but I'm going on Friday morning as soon as shift's over. Not a killing offense."

Did she know termination was near? Now with Tina and Howard dead, would the axe even fall? The fact the note was in the file proved Tina meant business. The bitch must have sent it up to HR immediately demanding it be filed. I wondered when she'd conveyed it upstairs and if Janet had been the courier.

I turned my attention back to the board. "I see I'm running relief tonight in Pit Two. You've got section one. Jim Collins is pitting and Nora is running relief for him. Probably going to be another slow night."

"Probably." She sent a speculative glance my way and frowned. "Is there something going on between you and Greg?"

"Maybe. I'm not sure yet. All I know is he didn't kill anybody." I glanced at my watch. "It's almost time. Think I'll hit the john. I'll try to give you a couple of extra minutes on your first break."

A relief's duties are to help change cards on the tables at the beginning of every shift. It's a time consuming task. Technically, the person running relief takes that first half hour as break time, but the truth is the break only lasts a few minutes. I'd barely have time to wash my hands before sending Cassie off.

"Tough news about Greg, huh?" Jim said when I signed on his last game.

"The cops are nuts. Greg didn't kill anybody." That refrain was getting old.

"I agree. I can't see him taking physical action. I'm sure the real killer will be found soon." He walked down the pit.

I wasn't so sure. According to a TV show, the first forty-eight hours of an investigation are crucial to solving the crime. Time was up for Tina and Janet's murders. And I didn't think the sheriff had other suspects on the horizon.

Worry and fear almost burned a hole in my stomach. Even if Wilcox released Greg, the sword of suspicion would still hang over him. And with the big bosses plus the gaming commission coming in tomorrow, his employment was in jeopardy. Casino owners these days, even if they were mob connected, wanted no hassles. The industry had cleaned up its act since the 1980s.

I paced up and down Cassie's section and checked my watch. Still ten minutes to go. The three-dollar blackjack table was full. Roulette had three players, and the rest of the games saw sporadic play. This was going to be a long night. Thank goodness I wouldn't be in any one section longer than half an hour. I stopped to chat with one of the players on a game, and then moved on.

Nora waddled into the pit to relieve Jim. Cassie was right behind her.

"Nothing going on," I told her. "All's quiet."

"Thank God."

Jim left the pit while I tapped out the dual-rate floor in the next section. The twenty-five-dollar table was empty as was one of the nickel games. A total of five players sat at the other two.

"I've never seen it so dead," Nora said as she stood leaning on the pit podium. "Even for a Tuesday. Maybe it's time to move on again. Get another new start. Mark my words, this place will look like a ghost town in another two months if that asshole sheriff doesn't figure out who did it—other than Greg, of course."

"Greg didn't kill anyone!" I was so tired of singing this tune.

She massaged the small of her back. "Yeah, well he's in the slammer for a reason."

"A lot of other people had a motive, you included."

"Me!" Her eyebrows pulled together in a deep scowl. "What the hell are you talking about?"

"You were always bad-mouthing Tina and Howard, not to mention the casino and how it's run."

"Everybody does that."

"Change hundred!" one of my dealers called out.

"Change it," I okayed before turning my attention back to Nora. "Tell me, exactly how many of these people did you know when you came here? Other than Howard and Jack, I mean."

She ceased rubbing her back and stared at me through narrowed eyes.

"What are you talking about?"

"Terence, Mississippi, is not a hotbed of casino

action or high rollers. In fact, it's kinda the bottom of the barrel. Greg knows a couple of floors on day shift from another time and place. People move around a lot."

"I told you, I worked with Jack several years ago, but that's it. I didn't even know Howard to speak of, and I don't know any of the other incompetents in this dump." She straightened. "Watch your games, Dallas. That's why you get paid. I'm going to harass that bitch Charlene for a while."

I stared as she walked down the pit. I shouldn't have questioned her. Now she'd clam up. I suspected she lied or at least hid something.

Jack, on the other hand, could confirm the information. I hadn't talked to him yet about Niagara Falls. Maybe I'd hit him with my knowledge both he and Nora knew Howard in New York. It might surprise an answer out of him.

Then I remembered something from the night Tina was killed. Nora had mentioned Tina "discussing" employee relations. Yet I didn't recall seeing her on the surveillance tape. Where had Tina told her this? Certainly not in the office. Did they meet backstage or somewhere more private? And was that all they discussed?

I relieved Charlene, and then took my first full break. I had my usual soft drink and candy bar, but sat at an out of the way table. I couldn't and wouldn't answer any more questions about Greg. Across the room, I spied Ralph doing the same. I rose and sauntered over to him.

"Hi, Ralph, how's it going?" I took a seat opposite him.

"Do you really care?"

I shrugged. "Sure. Don't remember having seen you the last couple of days."

"Sunday and Monday are my days off. Tina's death has me very upset. She was a good friend and talked to me. She wished more of the employees had liked her and treated her with respect. She did the best she could." He glared at me. "Why?"

"Hey, don't get all hostile on me. I was just curious."

He rose. "Yeah, well curiosity killed the cat, Dallas. Just remember that. And for the record, I think Greg Holland killed everyone."

With that, he stalked out of the room his tall, beefy frame rigid as steel. Was he still Tina's champion or just saying that? Had to be the latter. According to two sources, he'd been as good as fired. Yet, no mention had been found in his file. Tina hadn't had time to enter it, and Howard was too caught up in the chaos of her death to do anything about it before biting the big one himself.

The next relief rotation went well. It wasn't until midnight when the shit hit the fan.

I groaned when I walked in to relieve Cassie. Goofy and Daffy were playing roulette.

"Oh, no," I said, signing on one of the BJ games. "I don't need these two tonight."

"Thought you'd be pleased," Cassie said. "Came in about ten minutes ago. They play the same damned numbers and have only hit twice. He's eyeballed the camera a couple of times already. Good luck."

She left for her break, and I strolled up and down the section, staying as far away from the roulette table as possible. Goofy/Daffy glared at me whenever I came close. His wife, Daffy/Goofy, did the same. Tonight she was dressed in some kind of dress that resembled a slip. The spaghetti straps barely held up her sagging boobs. It was form-fitting and every bulge showed. He, of course, wore the usual paisley pants and green T-shirt.

I had almost made it through the half an hour when Carol, the roulette dealer called out, "Floor!"

Taking a deep breath, I approached the game. "Yes?"

"I want that damned laser turned off right now or I'm calling the gaming commission!" Goofy said through clenched teeth.

"Sir, that is a surveillance camera. Nothing more."

"I know a lot about technology. The dealer has a button she pushes to activate the laser and make the ball jump."

I really didn't need this bullshit. "For the last time, there is no button."

"Like hell! You're all a bunch of cheats."

Daffy curled her lip and sniffed. "I don't understand why you're still here. We complained to your boss about you the other night. You should be on the unemployment line."

I ignored her and concentrated on him. "If you think you're being cheated, why the hell do you play here?"

"I have an unbeatable system, and I'm going to prove it in spite of the laser." His voice had risen.

The anger that had gnawed inside me for the last couple of days would no longer be contained. I lost it.

"Your system is a pile of shit and as stupid as you are!" My voice topped his in decibel levels.

His wife sucked in an audible breath. "You can't talk to us that way! We're paying customers."

"Oh, shut up!"

Goofy stiffened his spine and glared. "I am going to break this casino!"

"Not on a twenty-five cent game, you cheapskate! You only bought in for ten bucks!"

"I'll have your ass for this!"

"And I'm going to kick it hard and long," his wife added.

"Try it, honey, and I'll sue. My uncle's a top-notch attorney in Memphis." I lied, but how would they know?

By now my dealer was laughing so hard she had to clench the edge of the table to remain upright. Players on other games stopped to stare at the commotion. Jim hustled down from the Stud section.

"What's going on here?"

"These two morons are convinced the surveillance camera is a laser and that we're cheating them. We've been through this a hundred times in the past. I've had it!"

"I want this woman fired! Now!" Daffy hollered. "She's rude and doesn't know the first thing about customer relations. The customer is always right."

"Dallas, I'll take care of this. Go watch your other games," Jim said in a calm tone.

Jim walked out of the pit and escorted the couple off to the side. I strode up and down, not even pretending to look at the tables. Cassie finally returned.

"Anything going on?" she asked as was the custom.

"You have no idea."

She gave me a funny stare as I moved on to the next section. A few minutes later she sidled up to me.

"Carol says you called them morons. Did you really?"

"And cheapskates! I *will* be getting disciplined if not fired, but I don't give a rat's ass. I've had it."

Cassie laughed. "Don't worry. I'm sure Jack will understand the circumstances. And if he doesn't you can always join me in Nevada."

Jim came back into the pit. Goofy and Daffy were gone.

"Jeez, Dallas, couldn't you have been just a little more diplomatic?"

"Oh, who cares? I suppose they're complaining to Jack at the moment."

"I'm afraid they insisted."

I used the rest of my hour in the pit to cool off. Before Charlene came back from her break, Jim walked down to the Stud section.

"Go see Jack on your break, Dallas."

"Yeah, yeah, whatever."

I didn't care that I may have bought permanent pink, but I was disgusted it might come at the hands of two assholes like Goofy and Daffy.

And if I get fired, how will that help Greg?

Chapter Sixteen

Back by popular demand, I walked into the office and stopped in front of the new secretary's desk. I still didn't know her name.

"Dallas Daniels to see Jack Mathias."

"He's waiting for you."

"Dallas, come on in," he called out in a weary tone.

Sighing, I did as he asked, and then stopped on the threshold. Sheriff Wilcox once again sat in a chair off to the side.

"Shut the door and have a seat, Dallas."

I obeyed reminded that I had done the same the night before. *Deja vu all over again.*

"I know the last few days have been rough on all of us, but did you have to call paying customers morons and cheapskates?" Jack asked.

"Seemed like a good idea at the time, and I refuse to apologize. They're a couple of nut cases."

"I know, but this time they put their complaint in writing. I had to comp them a full meal in the steakhouse. Right now, they're probably on the internet giving this place a zero rating along with a scathing review. I have no choice but to suspend you without pay for a couple of days. You have tomorrow and Thursday off. I need you here for the weekend nights, so the suspension begins Monday evening. Any questions?"

"Fine and no, I don't have any questions. I can use the peace and quiet. When I come back will you tell me to make it permanent?"

"I don't know yet. The head honchos are coming in tomorrow, so maybe I can sweep this under the rug. Just keep in mind, they may demand you leave."

"Yeah, yeah, whatever," I muttered again. Maybe I should use the time to look for another job. Nevada didn't sound bad. I'm sure Cassie had maintained her contacts over the years. She might be able to put in a good word for me with someone. I wondered if Greg would come with me.

I avoided looking at the sheriff, but his presence piqued my curiosity. Had he seen the tapes he'd requested from Billings?

Jack shook his head. "Just try to stay out of trouble for a while, will you? I don't need this right now. Go take your break."

"If you don't mind, Mr. Mathias, I'd like to speak with Miss Daniels privately, if I may," the sheriff said.

Jack rose. "You can use this office. I'm going to take a turn around the casino, and then get something to eat."

He left closing the door behind him. I turned toward Wilcox.

"Did you see the tapes?"

He nodded. "The guy entered the casino through the hotel entrance and went directly to the men's room. He exited out the main entrance. Cameras in the parking lot followed him toward The Southern Belle. We lost him when he went behind the bushes that separate the properties."

"What does that mean? That he was lying in wait

for somebody? Howard?"

"Looks that way. Whether or not it was Mr. Spivey, we aren't sure."

"Which means Greg didn't do it."

"It means someone else may have had a motive."

I leaned forward and glared. "Which means *he didn't do it!* Drop the charges. Let him go."

"I talked to the DA and told him what I'd seen. The charges have been dropped. I called the jail a while ago and had him released."

Relief rolled through me like a wave on the shore. Greg was free. I pulled my cell from my jacket pocket. Sure enough, a text message had come through while I was in the pit.

"I also have other news. The coroner has the cause of death for both Ms. Rosetti and Ms. Washington. It's all a lot of medical terms and such, but the upshot is they both died from a massive overdose of digitalis."

I jerked my head up from my cell screen. Where had I heard that recently? "Digitalis?"

"He gave it another name, but that's what it is."

"Isn't that a heart medication?"

Wilcox nodded again. "Used for heart failure or to regulate the heartbeat."

Jack! That's who'd mentioned taking digitalis!

"Sheriff, Jack Mathias takes that medication."

"I know. I told him the cause of death before you came in. He admitted taking it."

I thought back to that night. "But he wasn't feeling well the night of the murders. He left early, so he couldn't have done it. If he'd dumped a bunch of pills into the coffee pot, wouldn't Tina or Janet have croaked a lot sooner than they did? Maybe someone got a hold of his meds."

"Mr. Mathias is off the hook. According to the coroner, there was no pill residue in either the coffee cups or the pot. He thinks the medicine must have been in liquid form."

"Liquid? You mean like a kid's medication?" Cherry-flavored digitalis?

The sheriff shrugged and glanced at his watch. "He didn't say. I've got to go. Just thought you'd like to know."

I rose, eager to get out of the office and some place private to call Greg.

"Thanks, Sheriff. I appreciate you thinking of me."

We walked out together, me heading for the backstage area and he for the main entrance. I breezed past the break room and pushed through the doors into the parking lot. Leaning against a car, I called Greg. He answered on the second ring.

"Hello, gorgeous! I'm a free man!"

Tears formed in my eyes and rolled down my cheeks at the sound of his voice. "I know. I just heard. Congratulations."

"I have no idea why he suddenly turned me loose, but I'm not questioning it."

I laughed through my tears and told him what the sheriff had told me.

"Digitalis? You're kidding. By the way, the technical terminology is digoxin."

"How do you know that?"

"My dad took it for years, and in the liquid form, too. He'd just squeeze a couple of drops into his coffee and be set for the day. Any idea who the guy was on tape?"

"No, but I think I may have seen him before. Of course, that could also be the power of suggestion. Who knows?" I glanced at my watch. "Are you home now?"

"Yeah, just pulled in when you called."

"I'll come straight to your place after shift. There's more to tell, but I'm running short of time."

He laughed again. "I'll make breakfast, honey. The best ever! Oh, Lord, I can't wait for you to get here."

The implications of why made my heart beat faster and my stomach to do strange little flip-flops. I think I'd fallen deeper in love.

"Oh, this will cheer you up further. The ex-Mrs. Holland is no longer in the area. Seems the sheriff had a little chat with her about false accusations and suggested she might find employment somewhere other than Terence. She checked out of the motel and moved on."

"Thank goodness." The bitch was gone. Another worry out of the picture.

Getting a job in Terence where anybody who breathed got hired should have been easy, but sooner or later, the theft charge would trickle down the pipeline. Her casino employment days were over. If I were her, I'd dye my hair and wait tables in some obscure little town until the thugs wanting payback on the markers had given up.

It wasn't until I hung up that something the sheriff said jolted my memory. The guy on tape had walked toward the Belle parking lot. Suppose he'd parked there and come through the employee lot at the Casablanca to enter via the hotel entrance. Had the shadow I'd seen on Sunday night, and thought may have been stalking me, really have been this guy? The timing was close. I swallowed hard. Oh, shit! I may have seen Howard's killer. Had he seen me? I doubted it. He'd have been intent on his mission.

It didn't matter anyway. All I cared about was that Greg was free. My spirits soared.

I made my way back to the pit with a spring in my step. Four murders? Who cared? Suspension? So what? I figured Greg and I would be on the unemployment line together pretty soon. I had no idea where he'd go next, but I sure as hell wanted to be with him. Nevada?

"You look like you just got laid," Cassie said as I signed on her games. "Shit eating grin from ear to ear."

I laughed. "Comes close. I got suspended."

She gave me a funny look. "This I gotta hear."

"I'll tell you all about it when you get back from break and I'm pretending to watch section two."

Half an hour later, Cassie stood next to me at the end of her section while I gave her the lowdown on Greg.

"He's free? Dallas, that's wonderful. I take it you were suspended for the Goofy/Daffy incident. Carol told me she hadn't had a laugh like that in ages."

I confirmed the dealer's information. "I'm seriously thinking of looking for a new job during my time off. There's gotta be something out there I can do that pays more than minimum wage."

"You can answer a phone and I know you have enough computer skills to handle a receptionist's job."

"Maybe. Nevada doesn't sound half bad. Know anybody out there?"

"Lots of people. Dealing out there is fun. No matter where you go, the toke rate is double what you'd earn here."

"Looking better and better. Oh, and there's more." Excited, I told her about the coroner's report to the sheriff.

She paused for a second and okayed a color change on one of her tables.

"Digitalis? No kidding?"

"Yeah, and in the liquid form no less. Can you imagine? Other than Jack, I have no idea who else could be taking that med, do you?"

She shrugged. "I sure haven't seen or heard anything. I do remember that one floor supervisor who was diabetic and carried his insulin and syringe in his pocket."

"Me, too. His name was Matt or Mike or something like that. I couldn't help staring when I first saw him fill the needle. Thought he was shooting up something less legal right in the break room. Wonder what happened to him?"

"Moved on, I guess."

"Ladies, could you please at least walk around and pretend you're watching your games?" Jim said with a frown.

I obeyed, but didn't see the point. By this time next week, I'd most likely be history at the Casablanca.

The night wore on. I ate a light meal on my next break and resisted the temptation to call Greg again. That was so high school. Besides, he was probably in bed getting a decent night's sleep.

Yet I felt like a high school freshman again—all giddy with that teenage crush rush thing. Okay, it was silly, but I couldn't help it. My jealousy was gone with the departure of Bitch Central, and my fear of Greg ending our relationship this time around had faded into a not-so-fond memory. I could barely wait to get to his place and celebrate his freedom. And I did mean celebrate. The sheets would get a smoking workout this morning. No doubt about it.

I re-entered the pit for the last rotation of the night. Cassie had little to say and left as soon as I signed on. She looked tired. Working her days off as punishment for someone else's screw-up was typical of this place. I doubted she'd return to this little slice of hell either.

I actually watched my games since Jim watched me like a hawk. Surveillance had probably called down earlier on Cassie and me gossiping. Big deal. What were they going to do, suspend me? Fire me? Did I care? Nope.

I looked at my watch every few minutes willing the time to fly by. It didn't. It never does when you want it to. All I wanted was to get to Greg's—and celebrate.

Cassie returned and signed on her games with a scowl.

"Why the sour face?"

She shrugged. "I've got a lot on my mind."

I assumed she was thinking about her upcoming trip and possible permanent departure from Terence. If so, then this was her last night here.

Charlene collected the early out tonight. She barely waited for me to sign on her games before splitting without saying a word.

Ten more minutes. Ten more minutes and Graveyard would be here to put me out of my misery.

My relief was five minutes late. I had no idea who was relieving me, but tapped my foot at their tardiness. I was the last swing shift person left in the pit. I almost cheered when Rose Preston walked in and kept on coming my way.

"Looks pretty dead tonight," she said.

"It is. You've got one stud table, Let It Ride, and Three Card Poker."

"Hope I can stay awake," she said with a grin. "Go on, get out of here. Have a good day."

I didn't need to be told twice. I practically ran from the pit to the break room where I grabbed my purse from my locker and burst through the doors to the parking area and my car.

I deactivated my alarm and by reflex removed my cell phone from my pocket. I had another text from Greg. It had come through fifteen minutes ago.

Do NOT leave the casino! Stay in the break room and don't go anywhere alone. I'm on my way to you. I think I may know who killed Tina. I called the Sheriff to meet us there. Luv ya.

Luv ya? Was he serious? My silly hormones danced all over my body. Luv you, too, baby.

Then I looked at the main thrust of his text again. What? How did he know who killed Tina? And why would he be so concerned for me? I didn't know anything. Or did I? I sucked in a deep breath and dropped the phone back into my pocket. I had no idea what he was talking about, but the urgency couldn't be ignored.

I bit my lip. Did I know something, but not recognize what it was? Did it have something to do with the surveillance tapes?

With the sound of cars rapidly leaving the parking lot, I closed my eyes and tried to recall the last couple of days. Nothing stood out. Other than thinking the stranger in the men's john looked familiar, I couldn't pull up anything. And I never could identify who was in Howard's office the night I'd gotten written up. Yet, there had to be something glaring for Greg to get so het up.

I'd told only him about the tapes and my conversation with the sheriff. Well, and Cassie.

At my mental mentioning of Cassie, I remembered the incident in the break room with the two dealers dumping her purse and me helping collect the items. The bottle of eye drops stuck with me.

What was it Greg had said about his father and digitalis? *He'd just squeeze a couple of drops into his coffee and be set for the day.*

A prickling sensation covered my scalp and goose bumps rose on my arms. *Eye drops? Or digitalis?*

My mind snapped to the tape of Yolanda peering in the office door window, and then hurrying back to the slot machine seconds before Cassie walked out. What had she seen? Cassie dumping the bottle's contents into the coffee pot? *No, no, it can't be.*

"Oh my God," I whispered out loud. "And I even told her the cause of death."

Greg was right—I could be in danger. I'd wait for him inside. Footsteps sounded behind me.

I whirled with a yelp. Cassie stood near a lamp post staring at me.

Then I saw the gun in her hand.

Chapter Seventeen

I froze, staring at the gun. My gaze slowly traveled up to Cassie's face. The expression was calm, yet sad, with a hint of determination.

"Get in the car, Dallas."

"Cassie?" The word came out in a whisper.

"Don't make me shoot you. Please, just get in the car. We need to talk."

I didn't have much choice. Even though it was end of shift, my car was parked along the outer perimeter. I'd been late coming back from the Southern Belle earlier. Cars sped out of the lot. Not wanting to get shot and hoping I could talk her out of whatever she had in mind, I opened the door, slid behind the wheel, and, out of habit, fastened my seat belt. I reached for the door.

"Leave it open. Unlock the passenger side door and put your hands on your head where I can see them."

I complied.

"Good girl. Now don't move." She sidled around the front of the car, the gun barrel trained on me the whole time. Her gaze bored a hole in me as she opened the door and got in. She sat sideways in the seat, and stared, the gun never wavering.

"Wait a couple of minutes for more cars to leave," she instructed.

I closed my door and stared straight ahead through the windshield, my heart hammering. I licked my lips.

"They weren't eye drops, were they?"

"I knew the minute you told me about the liquid digoxin that the sheriff would subpoena medical records if possible. By the time he sees I was prescribed the medication, I'll be long gone. I have a sister living in Mexico. She's been after me for a while now to retire and join her. This seems like a good time to do it. I was afraid you'd remember about that bottle. For all I knew you'd read the label."

"And Yolanda?" The late cashier's name almost stuck in my dry throat.

"Sneaky, drunken bitch! Had the nerve to tell me she'd seen me tamper with the coffee pot. Demanded money. I told her I'd bring it by her place when shift ended. She was still drunk and made the mistake of turning her back on me. I grabbed that stupid bowling pin and cracked her head with it a couple of times, and then wiped my prints clean. The only reason that bottle was still in my pocket was because I was pissed at Tina and forgot to take my dose. On impulse, I just dumped it into the coffee pot. When you told me the cause of death, I figured you knew and were being more subtle about it than Yolanda."

Nausea rolled in my stomach. I swallowed hard to keep it there. "What are you going to do about me?"

She hesitated. "I'm thinking about it. I like you, Dallas."

That's comforting. She likes me. But I was pretty sure she was also going to kill me. *Was probably planning it in the pit that last rotation.* Greg and the sheriff were on their way. Could I distract and delay Cassie's actions long enough for them to arrive? *But what happens when they do?*

"Okay, start the car. Let's get out of here."

I inserted and twisted the key with shaking fingers. A sharp pain slashed across my chest. I had no idea what to do other than as she said.

I drove slowly out of the parking lot. "Why kill Tina?"

"I couldn't afford to lose this job. I need the benefits. She said if I went to Human Resources and made her look bad, I was fired. I didn't believe her." Cassie sighed. "Later, Tina told me she didn't appreciate me going over her head to HR. It made her look incompetent. I told her she was. We argued for a few minutes and the upshot of it was she told me not to bother coming back to the Casablanca when my trip was over. Said she'd had it with opinionated pit personnel and the sooner she cleaned house, the better the casino would be—or words to that effect. She then ordered me to come to her office after shift. She'd draw up termination papers and make it official. I was so fucking angry."

"She fired you for going to HR?" I said. "She can't do that."

"She could use any excuse she wanted," Cassie relied. "It's not like I haven't given her ample reasons in the past."

"Why are you taking digitalis?" I asked pulling onto the main road leading from the casinos to the highway.

"I was diagnosed with an irregular heartbeat last summer. All I needed was to keep this stinking job for another few years. Then I'd retire and Medicare would take care of everything. I'm too old to start over as a dealer. Dealing is drudgery. Even with my experience of close to forty years in the business, finding a new job in any casino would be a tough sell.

"The outer office was empty. Spivey was making his usual rounds of the casino, checking all the pits, the cashier's cage, the slot office. He always did that between one and two in the morning. I guess Janet was on break. Like I said, I was so angry when I saw the schedule before shift, I forgot to take my dose. Kept forgetting all through the night. I'm a creature of habit. I can't deviate from routine."

She inhaled a shaky breath before continuing.

"At any rate, when I came out of her office. I closed the door behind me. I stood there for a couple of seconds trying to come to grips with getting fired. The coffee pot was half full sitting on the warming burner. Then I remembered Tina's nightly stroll to the craps pit with her travel mug of coffee. I didn't stop to think. I just emptied the bottle into the pot. I didn't care if she lived or died."

"But you also got Janet in the bargain," I said.

"I'm truly sorry about Janet. I didn't even consider that she might pour a cup for herself. When I heard she'd died, I felt awful. I knew it was only a matter of time before somebody would find out I took digitalis."

Sweat dampened my palms and my hands slipped on the steering wheel.

"What about Howard?"

"Not me. I had an alibi for him. I was in the pit."

I'd forgotten about that. I licked my lips. "Look, Cassie, all you have to do is tell the sheriff you didn't know the medicine could kill her. You just thought it would make her sick. And it never occurred to you that Janet would also have coffee. A good lawyer will call it temporary insanity or something."

"And what about Yolanda?"

"You wiped the prints from the murder weapon. And Yolanda probably had a long list of enemies. With any luck, no one will ever know."

"Someone always knows. I parked right in front of her trailer."

"It was also four in the morning. Most people are asleep."

She was silent for a moment, still staring at me. "I'd still do jail time. At my age, that isn't much of an option even in a minimum security prison. No, I prefer a small beach town in Mexico."

I drove over the levee and stopped at the stop sign at its foot before moving on. Somehow, someway, I had to make her understand that another death would not help matters—especially if it was mine.

Then a spark of hope lifted my spirits. My headlights revealed Greg's car passing me. I chanced a glance in the rearview mirror. His brake lights came on. Seconds later, he pulled a U-turn and followed me. I slowed allowing him to catch up. Then he abruptly slowed, too, and dropped back again. Maybe he'd seen I wasn't alone. A sheriff's car flashed past us.

"Don't do anything stupid," Cassie warned. "Just ignore the cop car and keep on driving."

I shifted my frightened gaze to the rearview mirror again. Greg flashed his lights at the cop car. A moment later, it also made a U-turn and followed us. I breathed easier. At least help was close by.

"Look, Cassie, be reasona—"

"Shut up, Dallas. I'm tired of talk."

I ceased talking. Cassie's gun hand never wavered.

I chanced a look at her. She stared with a curiously blank expression, as though not seeing me. Was she visualizing her granddaughter's graduation? A Mexican beach? Her escape? My death?

The last thought made me want to throw up. Of course, she was planning my death. I was a loose end. One she couldn't afford to have remaining that way. She'd kill me, go back to work the next couple of nights, and then leave for California. No one would miss me because Wednesday and Thursday were my days off. No one except Greg. Had she thought about that in her panic? She knew Greg and I were seeing each other. Had she considered his reaction to not being able to contact me? She had no idea I'd told Greg about the digitalis. I had to let her know she wouldn't get away with killing me.

"Cassie…"

"Drive, Dallas." We approached another intersection. "Turn left up ahead."

She meant the old two lane highway. It had carried most of the traffic to and from Memphis and Terence when the casinos first opened. But drunks and fatal accidents had forced the construction of a new four lane highway further east. Now only locals used the old road.

"Cassie, what are you going to do?"

"I'm not sure yet. What you said makes sense. The part about what I tell the cops, I mean."

I glanced at her again. I wasn't the only one sweating. Tiny rivulets ran down her temples. She lied. She knew exactly what she was going to do. Her words were spoken to give me false hope and keep me under control.

A lot of country roads intersected the old highway—lonely, often deserted country roads. My friend and mentor planned on killing me. And when the deed was done, she'd drive my car back to the parking lot, leave it, then head for home in her own. It might be days before tape from the parking lot was reviewed. How soon someone stumbled across my body would determine that. And for all I knew, she planned on leaving for her trip tonight.

The first fingers of dawn streaked the eastern sky turning the darkness into a murky light. The cross road was just ahead. I slowed, flipped on my turn signal, and glanced in the mirror. Greg and the sheriff also slowed to a crawl. An oncoming delivery truck forced me to stop. Then an outrageous idea popped into my mind, but this was a do or die situation.

With a mental prayer, I waited until the headlights of the quick moving truck was just yards away, then stomped on the accelerator, jerked the wheel, and turned left in front of him.

Brakes shrieked. Cassie screamed as her body lurched against the door. Impact!

The airbag deployed as glass shattered and metal ripped. The shoulder strap dug into my body and the seat belt damn near cut me in half. The gun went off. Gunpowder stung my nostrils. The car spun and rolled. My head hit something, then snapped back and forth a couple of times. A searing pain slashed through my head and everything went black.

****

Strange beeping noises and the smell of disinfectant were my first conscious senses. I tried opening my eyes, but it was as if they'd been glued shut. I moaned and tried again. This time a sliver of light penetrated the darkness.

"Dallas? Dallas! Come on, honey, talk to me. Open those beautiful baby blues."

Greg's voice told me I was alive. "Greg? Where…what…?"

"You're in the Terence County Hospital, but you're going to be all right. Bumps, bruises, and some cuts, but all right. Okay?"

His voice sounded thick as if he had something stuck in his throat. His hand clutched mine and brought it to his damp face where he kissed it. Tears?

"And my eyes are brown," I said knowing I didn't make much sense.

"Whatever," he replied with a laugh.

"Cassie?" I whispered.

"Later, honey. We'll talk later. Doctor, she's awake!"

A man in a white coat stepped around the curtain. "Welcome back to the real world, Miss Daniels. My name is Doctor Travis."

He promptly shooed Greg out and examined me. I was slowly coming to full consciousness.

"I take it I'm going to live?" That was a strong statement, considering.

"You've got some nasty cuts on the left side of your head from the window glass, and a mild concussion. All in all, I'd say you were damned lucky."

"And the woman with me?"

He ignored my question and jammed a thermometer into my mouth. "We're going to keep you twenty-four hours for observation. The sheriff is waiting outside to ask you some questions. Feel up to it?"

I nodded. I glanced around the tiny emergency room space while waiting patiently until the doctor removed the thermometer. Wires ran from my body to several machines. One beeped rhythmically. Another dripped fluid into a tube in my arm. I touched my head. Bandages swathed it like a cap. I was glad no mirrors were available. My whole body hurt.

He moved the curtain and signaled someone outside. The sheriff walked in.

"Don't keep her too long," the doctor said before leaving.

Sheriff Wilcox stood at the foot of the bed, his arms crossed over his chest. "How are you feeling?"

"Other than the headache from hell and hurting like a son of a bitch from my hair to my toenails, just peachy."

He removed his Smokey hat and wiped the inside with a handkerchief. "I can't decide if what you did was incredibly brave or incredibly stupid."

"The way I feel right now, I'll go for stupid." Tears welled. I bit my lip and gazed into his somber eyes. "Cassie's dead, isn't she?"

He nodded. "Direct impact on the passenger side door at close to fifty miles an hour—and she wasn't wearing a seat belt. Killed instantly."

I sniffed and wiped the tears from my cheeks. I'd killed my friend and even though she'd planned on doing the same to me, I still felt sorrow.

"And the truck driver? Is he all right?"

"Shaken up with a few cuts and bruises, but he's fine."

"Thank God."

"It was an old delivery truck with the cab sitting high above the engine." He replaced the hat on his head and took a small tape recorder from his pants pocket, laying it on a rolling dinner tray nearby and pushed a button. "You ready to tell me what happened?"

I inhaled a deep, shaky breath and told him the whole story. "I never suspected Cassie for a moment. I was so excited about Greg being free, I'm afraid I just spilled my guts to her about everything. She figured you'd find out about the digitalis sooner or later."

"I'm not sure we'd have had enough evidence to access everyone's medical records, but then guilty people often assume we have more than we do."

Just like she assumed I'd read the bottle contents and was being subtle about blackmail?

"Is there anything else?"

Weariness swept over me. All I wanted was to sleep and forget the past few hours. "No, that's it, at least for now."

He turned off the recorder. "When they spring you from here, come into the station and you can add anything else you remember. We'll type it up and you can sign it."

"Okay. Will there be any charges against me for reckless driving?"

"Probably, but I'm sure that on my recommendation they'll be dismissed. The delivery company might try to sue you."

I snorted. "Fat chance. I don't have any money. What was he delivering?"

The sheriff grinned. "Vegetables to the Southern Belle. Have a good rest and I'll see you soon."

"Swell, I was almost done in by a load of

cabbages."

He left and I closed my eyes letting tears of grief for my friend flow. In my mind I saw Cassie's laughing face—the kind she often wore in the break room before murder took over her agenda. Happy, carefree, full of fun. That's how I'd always remember her.

****

I awoke to a hospital room full of natural light. To my right, a machine still beeped and a bag hanging from a stand continued to drip into my arm. I'd been moved to a private room shortly after the sheriff had left. Throughout the morning, nurses woke me at regular intervals making sure my concussion wasn't permanent.

A soft snore made me look to the left. Greg slept in a chair wedged into the corner near the window. A hospital issue-type blanket covered him. He didn't look the least bit comfortable. Just his presence gave me an old-fashioned thrill. Warmth spread from the pit of my stomach through the rest of my body.

A nurse came into the room. "Oh good, you're awake. How are you feeling?"

Over in the corner, Greg jerked awake with a snort, threw off the blanket, and sat up rubbing his eyes.

"As good as can be expected. How long do I have to have this stuff attached to me?"

She made a notation on my chart at the foot of the bed. "Shouldn't be too much longer. The doctor will be in shortly. Are you hungry? It's only three o'clock. Lunch is over, but I think I can scrounge up something for you to munch on."

My stomach grumbled at the word food. "That sounds great."

She left and I turned my head toward Greg. "Hello, handsome. I take it you've been here all night." I glanced at the window. "Or morning and afternoon as the case may be."

He smiled, rose and came to sit on the edge of the bed. He leaned over and kissed me lightly on the lips.

"Of course, I stayed. I had a lousy night's sleep, but it was better than anything I'd get at home. There I'd simply toss and turn worrying."

"I'm sure you monitored the nurses whenever they came into the room."

"Naturally. Had to know what was going on with my girl."

My heat level rose. "Your girl?"

He kissed me again, a little longer and harder. "Yeah, my girl."

Before we could explore that answer, the doctor breezed in.

"Good afternoon, Miss Daniels. How're you feeling?" He picked up my chart and glanced at it.

"Not bad, considering. When can I go home?"

"I'd like to keep you overnight, just to be sure that concussion is on the road to recovery."

"My body's sore, but my headache's gone, at least mostly."

"Make a deal with you. I'll send you down for a CAT scan, and if all is well, I'll send you home first thing in the morning."

I was about to protest when Greg jumped in. "That sounds reasonable, Dallas. That'll make it a full twenty-four hours. I've heard stories about people with head injuries being fine one minute and dead the next. Why tempt fate?"

I could see from the determined look on both their faces I would lose this argument. "Oh, all right, but can I have real food for dinner, like pizza or a burger and fries?"

The doctor winced. "You're rejecting our fine hospital cuisine? I'm hurt."

Greg laughed. "I'll be the waiter and make sure to bring a salad along with it."

He laughed along with Greg. "I guess that'll be okay. Just try not to let the smell of appetizing food out of the room. Can't have the rest of the patients inciting a riot."

When he left, Greg turned to me. "What do you want for dinner?"

"Pizza! Pepperoni, mushroom, black olives, and anchovies."

His eyebrows rose. "Anchovies?"

"You heard me, buster. I love those little suckers."

"Oddly enough, so do I. Your wish is my command."

Before I could comment on his use of clichés or his good taste in food, the nurse brought in a tray and set it on the rolling table.

"This is it for now. I'll see what I can order from the kitchen for dinner."

"The doctor has okayed outside food for tonight," I said quickly.

"Lucky you." She chuckled and left.

The tray consisted of a carton of fruit punch, banana pudding, vanilla wafers, and an apple.

I found the remote control and pushing a button raised the head of the bed. Greg maneuvered the tray over my lap. Cautiously, I opened the various lids and packages.

He pulled the chair up to the side of the bed and watched me eat the meager offering.

"That pizza's sounding damned good. This stuff takes the edge off, but I'm freaking hungry," I mumbled through a mouthful of pudding.

"I'll head for home in a while, shower, change clothes, and bring you the feast you so deserve by six o'clock, your highness."

"Smart ass." I laughed, and then sobered remembering my friend. I put my spoon down and stared at the wall opposite me. "Poor Cassie. I feel so bad. I mean, I never had a clue. Is…is that who you meant in your text?"

Greg heaved a sigh and nodded. "I'd gone to bed, but couldn't get to sleep. You telling me about the digoxin as the poison made me think about my father. The older he got the more often my mom had to monitor his dosage. Make sure he didn't forget to take it. I remembered the time, she went out of town overnight and he forgot. We had to take him to the hospital. He was exhausted, shaking, pale. A quick dose solved the problem.

"Then I remembered Cassie the night Tina and Janet died. She exhibited the same symptoms. And I'd once seen her add a couple of drops of something to a cup of coffee in the break room. She must have taken her dose just before shift so she wouldn't have a problem throughout the night."

"She told me she forgot that night because of her argument with Tina."

Greg shook his head. "It didn't strike me at the time, but the more I thought about it, the more I was convinced the digoxin had come from her. I called the sheriff immediately and texted you."

"I didn't read it until I got to my car. Then I remembered a lot of things, too." I gave him the story of the spilled purse, Yolanda's strange behavior on the surveillance tape, and Cassie's confession in the car.

"Yolanda got greedy. I guess Cassie was so scared by Tina and Janet dying, she felt she had to silence Yolanda as well," he said.

"And me when she thought I knew something, too." I bit my lip to stop the tears from welling. It didn't work. They spilled over and down my cheeks.

Greg shoved the tray from in front of me and sat on the bed where he cradled me in his arms.

"Don't cry, honey. What Cassie did was wrong, but she had reached a breaking point. We all do. Most of us, however, don't follow through on thoughts of murder."

"And she never got to see her granddaughter graduate from Cal Tech. She was so proud!"

My statement sounded silly, but it was all I could say. I had unmasked a killer, but at a terrible price.

I clung to him and sobbed out my fear and sorrow. His arms tightened as he crooned soothing words in my ear. This was a man I could trust forever. And I wanted forever.

Chapter Eighteen

"Let's swing by the sheriff's office on the way home," Greg suggested as we drove away from the hospital.

We'd enjoyed a great pizza, and I'd passed a restful night. The doc had finally sprung me. It was nine in the morning and I was on my way home to grab some clothes. Greg had all but insisted I move in with him. I didn't put up an argument.

"That's fine with me. I have to sign my statement anyway."

At the police station, the sheriff saw us immediately.

"Glad to see you aren't any worse for wear," he said as we took seats in front of his desk.

Easy for him to say. I looked as though my next job would be at the carnival midway. Chunks of hair had been shaved from the left side of my head. Stitches showed in the stubble. Thank God, my arms and the airbag had spared my face any glass cuts from when the car had rolled. I still hurt like a son of a gun and had the bruises to prove it. I'd never realized seat belt contusions were so readily defined or painful.

"I'm feeling much better, Sheriff. I'm here to sign that statement now."

He pulled a tape from a file folder and inserted it into a recorder, then pushed play. My voice from the emergency room came through. I was amazed at how slow I talked and the occasional slurring of the words. Must have been the meds they'd given me—or the concussion.

"Anything you want to add?" Wilcox asked when the tape played out.

I added a few extras about what Cassie had said in the car.

He nodded, removed the tape from the machine, and stood. "I'll have this typed up and you can sign it. Be back in a moment."

"Is there any news on Howard's death?" Greg inquired when the sheriff returned.

"No. We may never find the culprit."

We had only solved three of the murders. "Greg, have you seen the surveillance tapes from Sunday night?" I turned to the sheriff. "Maybe he can ID the guy."

Wilcox shrugged. "Can't hurt."

He showed us into the viewing room and popped the tape into the VCR. We watched the images from the men's room first, then the one from the hotel entrance and parking lot.

When they ended, Greg sat back with a frown. "I've seen that hat somewhere before."

"But you don't recognize the man?" the sheriff said.

"The physique looked familiar to me, but with that coat it's almost impossible to say."

"It was a disguise all the way," I chimed in. "And I don't think it was a woman. No woman I know would wear a hat like that in public. And whoever this is has perfect posture. Almost military like."

Something eluded my memory, but I couldn't nail down what.

"Quiet for a moment, please. Let me think." Greg rubbed his chin and closed his eyes. Only the ringing of phones in the distance broke the silence. Finally, he opened his eyes.

"It was quite a while ago. I'm not sure exactly when, but I think it may have been last winter. I remember being in the car before shift. I'd parked on the outer perimeter. It was dark, I do know that. I looked up through the windshield and saw someone in that hat heading for the employee entrance."

"You saw the hat? That's all?" the sheriff asked with a stern look.

"The only reason I remember it is the wearer passed under a light post. At the time I thought the hat looked silly—like an Indiana Jones wannabe."

"The employee entrance," I murmured. "That means someone who works, or worked, here killed Howard. Which means whoever it was *did* wait specifically for him in the john." Once again, Yolanda's image came to mind.

I stared at the still image paused on the TV. Could it be her? Maybe, maybe not. Either way, I knew this person. I had to. But nothing was coming through in the form of an identity. Maybe the knock on the head had scrambled my brains more than I'd thought. I told them about my experience in the parking lot on Sunday night.

"You did that after I warned you not to go anywhere alone?" Greg asked in a stern voice.

"You said within the casino. I was in the parking lot."

"Same difference."

The sheriff held up his hand. "Can you argue about this later? Do you recognize the hat, Ms. Daniels?"

I shook my head. "No, not at all. All I heard were footsteps and all I saw was a shadow. I certainly couldn't make an ID based on that."

I refocused my attention back to the screen. That straight posture, the tall frame stuck in my mind. Where had I seen it before? Yolanda hadn't walked that way. She clomped like every step killed a cockroach. I closed my eyes and thought over the last week of work. Nothing. I was about to give up when it hit me.

"Oh my God!" I said with a gasp, my hand clutching my throat.

"What?" Greg and the sheriff said simultaneously.

"Ralph!"

"Ralph?" Greg echoed.

"Ralph who?" Wilcox barked.

"Ralph Klinger. Oh God, it all makes sense."

"Explain yourself, Ms. Daniels."

"You interviewed him and probably caught him in a lie about the night of Tina and Janet's murders."

I reminded the sheriff about what Anne and Yolanda had overheard in Howard's office that evening. Plus, he and Howard had had a chat over by the buffet table, and later Ralph had been sitting alone—right next to the unused silverware.

"I'll bet steak knives were included in one of the bins. And, old Ralph had military experience. That explains the perfect posture."

Sheriff Wilcox nodded. "Miss Harris never mentioned she'd overheard anything. I'll pull his file and get right on it."

"Plus he was off the night of Howard's murder,

would know where to park at the Southern Belle, and to cut through the Casablanca employee parking lot to get to the hotel entrance," I crowed in triumph.

"And then make his escape from the main doors back over to the Belle," Greg finished.

The chief law enforcer of Terence County, Mississippi, rose and smiled. "Thank you for helping. Both of you. Now go home and get some rest. I'll keep you up to date on what happens."

We left and headed north.

"We did it!" I exclaimed. "We solved the murders!"

"And our thanks will likely be the unemployment line. I wonder what the big boys from headquarters are doing right now."

My enthusiasm waned. Yeah, we had solved the crimes, but suddenly my financial future looked dim.

****

Greg and I walked into the break room on Friday evening. All conversation stopped as people stared. Without looking anyone in the eye, we made our way to the soft drink vending machine. Gradually, the sound level rose. Choosing a table, we sat and nodded to three day-shift dealers on break. They glanced at each other and promptly left.

"Well, at least we have the table to ourselves," he said opening the can and taking a sip. "Are you sure you want to be here?"

To the best of our knowledge, we both still had our jobs. Our final day and night off had been spent in bed. In spite of my sore muscles, we'd made love more times than I could count. I no longer dealt in fantasies. Reality rocked.

"I feel fine. Great, continuous sex must have healing properties."

He choked, swallowed, and then grinned. "Shame we can't bottle it."

"What a concept. Besides, I need to work. As of Monday, I'm suspended. I have the feeling I won't be back."

Before he could answer, Nora wandered up.

"So, Cassie did it, huh? I don't blame her. They'd screwed her for the last time. I liked Cassie. She was fun, sarcastic, and knew her job. I'm sorry she's dead."

"I am, too," I replied. "She was a good friend."

I still had a hard time believing I had killed my best friend. It was a terrible thing to assimilate into my mind.

Nora stared. "You look like hell."

I'd combed my shoulder length hair to cover as much of the shaved area on my head as possible. I touched it now.

"Yeah, but it beats the alternative."

In an uncharacteristic move, Nora placed her hand on my arm. "Hey, Dallas, you did what you had to do. She may have been your friend, but she was going to kill you."

My throat closed. I couldn't speak and sipped from my soda can instead. The silence lengthened until I finally had to ask, "Nora, the night Tina died you said she'd complained about how you treated Charlene, yet you never showed up on the surveillance tape going to the office. How come?"

"Bitch cornered me in the hallway outside the break room. She lectured me where anybody passing could hear. Pissed me off royally. I told her to cram it."

"So how did the sheriff know to keep you after the murders?"

"Meticulous bitch couldn't remember shit about what she'd done or said, so she wrote herself sticky notes. Had 'em stuck all over her fucking desk. The cops read it and added my name to the list of fun-seekers."

Greg leaned forward. "Nora, there's still something that's bugging us. Only you and Jack have the answer."

"Yeah, what's that?" She eyed him with a cautious look.

"What happened up in Niagara Falls?"

She lowered her gaze to the table top. "I have no idea what you're talking about."

"You, Jack, and Howard all worked together at the same casino in Niagara Falls," I reminded her.

"And when you all came here you received either promotions or salaries way beyond the industry standards," Greg added. "I'm especially curious about Howard's leap from Food and Beverage Manager to Casino Manager."

Nora hunched her shoulders, pressed her body forward, and answered in a low tone. "How the hell did you get that information?"

"Let's just say we know and leave it at that," I said.

She fiddled with a discarded straw wrapper someone had left on the table, and then sighed.

"It was seven or eight years ago. Jack was a pit manager, I floored, and Howard ran the bar and its personnel. One night this little shit comes in with some babe, sits at one of my tables, buys in for a couple of thousand bucks, and proceeds to be an arrogant pain in the ass from the get go. Kept bragging about how his

242

old man was some Chicago bigwig and owner of a couple of casinos.

"We ignored him until he started winning. And I mean winning. By two in the morning, the asshole was into us for close to a hundred grand. That's when the trouble began."

"What kind of trouble?" I asked.

"Suddenly, this little cocktail waitress begins showing up every five minutes with drinks. The arrogant kid downs them like water and his girlfriend is so loaded she almost passes out on the table."

"Let me guess, word came down from the shift and/or casino manager to get him drunk so he'd lose," Greg said.

Nora nodded. "Jack and I were told to keep an eye on him and report when he was tapped out."

"That's despicable," I told her.

Greg cocked his head and shrugged. "But it happens. Go on, Nora."

"So, the kid starts losing. We got back all but about ten grand. The only reason we didn't get that is because the babe puked all over the table and the game had to stop. They left. Two miles from the casino, he wraps his car around a tree killing the girl. He came out of it with cuts and bruises, but was arrested for DUI.

"The casino was scared to death of lawsuits *and* the gaming commission. Enter Howard Spivey."

Greg sat back and stared. "He was a former New York City cop and had connections."

"Bingo. He suggested destroying the surveillance tape from that table, and if anyone asked, say the camera was malfunctioning. The casino is off the hook. Meanwhile, the kid's father arrives along with a high-priced attorney. I don't know what went down, but the kid got off with a ridiculously light sentence—probation and community service or something."

"So how did you all end up here?" I asked.

"The casino considered us a liability. They suggested we all leave, but gave us substantial bonuses for doing so. Out of sight, out of mind, and if there was any kind of a trial, we'd be gone. Fast forward a year. Howard finds out the father is part owner of the soon-to-open Casablanca casino. He applies for the position of casino manager, and lo and behold, nails it down."

"Karnac," Greg said.

"Yeah."

"We always speculated he must have blackmailed someone into giving him the job. Same with Tina," I mused.

Nora waved her hand. "Tina got the job because her father and Karnac were old friends."

"And you?" I added.

She shot me a defensive look. "Hey, I'm not stupid. Word travels fast when a new joint opens. As soon as I heard Howard was casino manager, my resume hit his desk. Same with Jack."

"In other words, you both blackmailed Howard. He okayed enormous salaries and promotions down the line," Greg said with a curled lip.

"That's the nature of the business," she shot back.

"No it's not!"

Nora rose. "Go to hell, Holland. You wanted to know the connection. That's it. Now piss off."

"Oh wow," I said as she stalked from the room.

"I always said there was something fishy about this place. Now I know why. The stench is overwhelming."

The break room phone rang. A dealer answered, listened for a minute, and then hung up before calling out.

"Hey, Greg, Dallas. Jack wants to see both of you up in the second floor conference room right away."

I glanced at my watch—six fifty-five. "Now what?"

Greg shrugged. "Might be the end of the line for us."

"Or a big, fat raise. With this place, there's no telling."

We entered the conference room. Jack, Dave Billings, and three other men sat at the table.

"Dallas, Greg, have a seat, please," Jack said not making eye contact.

This didn't sound good. We sat.

"First of all, I'd like to introduce you to Robert Hoskins, Carl Prescott, and Joseph Karnac, the owners of the Casablanca Casino and Resort."

My attention focused on Karnac. Short, balding, and built like a bowling ball, he sat back and chomped on an unlit cigar. Acknowledgments were murmured all around.

"How are you feeling, Dallas?" Jack asked.

"A little sore, but I'm fine."

He turned his gaze onto Greg. "I may as well get this over with. Greg, you are a good pit manager, but your attitude leaves a lot to be desired. You're constant criticism and sarcastic comments in the break room seemed never-ending. Howard and Tina were concerned about employee morale. In the past year you've received no less than six reprimands. It's time for you and this casino to part ways."

My heart sank. Greg was gone. I was sure to be next.

"You simply beat me to saying the same thing. I had my resignation all written out on a roll of toilet paper."

"It's that attitude that has brought you to this," one of the owners, not Karnac, said.

Greg shrugged with a derisive snort. "I don't give a shit anymore, gentlemen. No pun intended."

Jack turned his attention back to me. "Dallas, we need you to clear up something, too."

Billings cleared his throat. "We have surveillance tape of you entering Human Resources after hours a few nights ago. Care to explain?"

Uh-oh. Busted. I gave them my carefully prepared story about leaving a note.

"We know about the note. One of the employees up there found it on her desk. You spent twenty-seven minutes in there. It doesn't take that long to write a note. What were you doing?"

"I waited around, hoping someone would show up. When they didn't I left."

"The housekeeper who let you in says you told her you were a new hire and had locked yourself out."

I had no answer for that.

Jack sighed. "Roberta also said it looked as if someone had tampered with her files."

"Wasn't me."

"I think it was," Billings continued. "It doesn't matter whose files you looked at. What matters is you did it."

"In view of this, we have no choice but to terminate your employment here, too," Jack informed me. "Your separation papers are being drawn up now. They'll be ready for your signatures tomorrow afternoon."

Tomorrow? They were pushing this through fast. I suppose I should have been crushed or at the very least, angry, but somehow, like Greg, I just didn't give a shit. Maybe the whole sleazy business had finally come home to roost with the message it wasn't the career for me.

I opened my mouth to let give them a scathing reply as to how this casino had been run when Greg squeezed my hand. I closed it again. No sense in admitting I knew what was in those files.

"Is that all?" Greg asked in a cool tone.

Jack nodded. "That's it. Sorry about how things worked out. Please turn in your badges."

We left the room and the casino without saying a word. Cleaning out our lockers took a whole five minutes.

"Where should we go to celebrate?" Greg asked with a smile stopping beside his car. My rental was just a few spaces over.

"Since we're both out of jobs, may I suggest some place cheap?"

"Suppose I stop at that Chinese take-out joint down the road from me?"

"Works for me."

"Meet you at my apartment."

Half an hour later, we sat down to General Tsao's Chicken, fried rice, egg rolls, and an order of crab rangoons.

As I chewed the spicy concoction, I speculated on my shaky future. And what would Greg do? He'd already said Terence was the end of the road.

"So, Dallas, what's next on your agenda?"

"Not sure, but something will come along. It always does."

"I mean your life agenda. Where do you see yourself ten years from now?"

I put my chopsticks down and stared him straight in the eye about to admit something I'd never told anyone before. It was my secret dream and had been for years. With my feelings for Greg now solid in my heart, I decided this was a good time to open up. I just hoped he wouldn't laugh.

"I see a house—not a mansion, just a nice little house—with a white picket fence and a big backyard. I want a master bathroom and a walk-in closet. I want a husband with a nine-to-five job. I want a whole passel of kids playing in that back yard. I'd like to be a stay-at-home mom, but am willing to work if I have to. I want the all-American dream."

He didn't laugh, but did have a serious expression on his face. Had I scared him with my vision? Was he about to say, "So long, Dallas, have a nice life"? Could he accept my wants, too? His life had been so footloose. Did the idea of staying in one place sound boring and predicable? God, I hoped not. I loved him and would give the world to have him on the same life page as me.

He placed his chopsticks next to his plate with a precise movement and pushed the plate back. He didn't look at me for a long moment. A bubble of sadness grew in my chest. Tears threatened.

Oh God, he's going to brush me off—again.

Finally, he leaned his arms on the table and gazed into my eyes. His expression was guarded and I couldn't read one damned emotion. I hoped I could take the heartbreak sure to come my way without begging and making a fool of myself.

"Did you know I majored in Accounting in college?"

Accounting? What the hell did that have to do with anything? I swallowed the ever growing lump in my throat and, unable to speak, shook my head.

"Yep. Math always came easy to me. About six months before I graduated, a bunch of my fraternity brothers and I went to the casinos in Atlantic City."

Fraternity brothers? Holy cow. I had no idea he was so...so...I couldn't think of the right word. Educated? Social? Just plain smarter than me? I hadn't read anything about it in his HR file, and wasn't about to admit I'd seen it.

"There I discovered I had a knack for counting cards, figuring out payouts, and estimating odds. I was hooked on casino life. I wanted the glamour, the glitz, but knew being a player wasn't for me. So, as soon as I had my degree in hand, I went to dealer school. That was twenty years ago."

I cleared my throat. "I had no idea."

"How do you feel about Pittsburgh?"

"Pittsburgh!" Where the hell had this come from?

"My older brother owns several furniture stores in the area. He's been after me for years to join him. I'm sure I can take a few refresher courses and get up to accounting speed pretty fast. I may even go for a CPA title. It's never too late."

"Greg, what are you trying to say?" I had to ask, because damned if I knew.

He reached across the table, took my hand, and

raised it to his lips. "Come with me, Dallas. We'll get your house and picket fence. My brother and his wife have four kids. They can fill that big back yard until we have munchkins of our own."

I couldn't help it. Tears spilled over and ran down my cheeks. "You do realize marriage comes into play, don't you?"

He smiled, his gray eyes held a gentle look. "I know. Wouldn't have it any other way."

"And you're not afraid of being bored staying in one place for the rest of whatever?"

"It's time I settled down and established roots. I can think of no one I'd rather do that with than you. I love you, Dallas. I have for a long time. It took murder and mayhem to make me see it. Will you marry me?"

"Of course!" I sobbed. "I love you, too, and Pittsburgh sounds beautiful."

He rose, came around the table, and pulled me up into his arms. His lips crashed down on mine. With a quick movement, he picked me up and carried me to the bedroom. I'd never been so happy. My vision was his vision. That was all I needed to know.

gaming commission in the first place. I liked to think that in one last act of revenge, it had been Cassie.

I even confessed my fantasy life to my new husband who chuckled.

"Years in the business taught me to use my peripheral vision. Every once in a while I'd catch you looking at me with a sexy expression on your face. It gave me hope, since I was having a few fantasies of my own concerning you. The platonic thing just wasn't working."

I had to laugh. "And to think I almost didn't go to that stupid party."

Greg's brother was thrilled at the prospect of gaining an accountant for his businesses, and sent congratulations on our marriage. He sounded like a nice guy. I couldn't wait to meet him and his family.

We packed our meager belongings, loaded them into a van and with Greg driving, headed east. I'd miss Memphis. Even though it was my hometown, my family had long since scattered. Maybe we'd visit someday, but I doubted it.

As I followed the van in his car, I couldn't keep my mind off Cassie. The guilt at causing her death would always be with me. I still missed her guiding advice, her sense of humor, and kindness to a new dealer. I would always miss her and think of her in those terms. Cassie as a killer was the act of a desperate woman.

However, without her actions, Greg and I may never have found each other—may never have discovered we had the same vision. And for that I was grateful.

"Thank you, Cassie," I said out loud. "Rest in peace."

I drew a deep breath and followed the red-and-white truck with my future in it. Pittsburgh. It didn't matter I knew next to nothing about the city. I was heading home.

A word about the author...

Suzanne was born and raised in Indianapolis, Indiana, but has had the pleasure of living in several states throughout her adult life.

During her college years at Ball State University she majored in History, and was the only student in the dorm who actually enjoyed writing term papers.

She has two grown sons and is blessed with six grandchildren, four boys and two girls.

Currently, she and her husband live in Ft. Lauderdale, Florida, with dogs Lucky and Liza, taking advantage of year-round warm weather, the beach, and all that goes with it.

She loves sharing her fantasies with readers and looks forward to meeting her fans.

Other Suzanne Rossi titles
available from The Wild Rose Press, Inc.:

ALONG CAME QUINN, January 2010
ALL IN THE FAMILY, May 2010
A TANGLED WEB, August 2010
NEARLY DEPARTED, December 2010
HEAR NO EVIL, June 2012
THE REUNION, October 2013
DEADLY INHERITANCE, December 2013
THROUGH MY EYES, coming soon

Epilogue

I gazed at the simple gold band on the ring finger of my left hand with a sense of wonder that left me breathless. I'd been Mrs. Gregory Holland for a whole week. It had been quite a week.

The day after Greg had popped the question, the sheriff dropped by to confirm the arrest of Ralph Klinger for the murder of Howard Spivey. Howard had officially fired Ralph right in the conference room the night of Tina and Janet's deaths. I remembered how he'd wiped his eyes and thought it had been grief for Tina. I also remembered the look on his face. I thought he'd looked frightened, but inside he must have been furious. All those years of being Howard and Tina's stooge had just gone up in smoke. No more attaboys, no more promotions, no more goodies on the side from Tina, no more anything.

"We got a search warrant and found the hat and the coat in his bedroom closet. Confronted with the evidence, he cracked. He admitted grabbing the steak knife and coming back the next night to wait for Howard. He hid in a stall until Howard was—uh, busy—rushed up, planted it in his back and left. We found some stains likely to be blood on the coat."

Apparently, Howard had forgotten to send the word up to Human Resources about the firing before he was killed. Incompetent right down to his own death.

I wondered if Ralph would buy a needle in the arm since he'd obviously planned to kill Howard, or if he'd spend the rest of his life in prison as someone's new best friend, and then shrugged. I knew I had the wrong attitude, but didn't really care.

At the Casablanca, nothing much had changed. A new casino manager was being brought in from Atlantic City. Jack was promoted to shift manager and Nora to full pit, taking over Greg's job as soon as she returned from maternity leave. Payments from Karnac for keeping his kid out of the slammer in Niagara Falls? Probably. However, neither Nora nor Jack was stupid enough to take it any further than that. A good solid job with reasonable pay would do the trick.

That bitch Charlene had made dual-rate pit. I'm glad I wasn't there anymore. Besides, with a competent casino manager now in place, how long would Charlene last? Maybe the place would be run better, but I doubted it and really didn't care about that either.

Greg's PI friend in Atlantic City confirmed most of what Nora had told us concerning Karnac's kid. Daddy had kept the little jerk on a tight leash until finding him a job in one of the casinos he owned. The position? Food and Beverage Manager. It was the ultimate irony.

The gaming commission met with the owners and eventually decided disgruntled employees had been responsible for everything. Rumor had it they had reprimanded the owners for lax oversight. Management had agreed and swore the new casino manager was highly experienced. From what I'd heard, the Casablanca was once again full of suckers who couldn't wait to lose their money.

We never did discover who'd complained to the